PIRATES!
You Guys?

E.T. McAllen

Book one of the *Pirates!* series.

Cover and interior design by the Nellacm L'rae Studios.

First Printing, 2017

ISBN: 978-0-9984999-1-8 (ebk)
ISBN: 978-0-9984999-0-1 (pbk)

Solipsismia Books
Austin, Texas, U.S.A.

Solipsismia Books is an imprint of Ilikas Publishing.
Contact: publish@ilikas.com

10 9 8 7 6

Translations

For the comfort of the reader, this series of adventures is translated into Earth-standard English. Frankly, the hundreds of spoken and written languages involved in this series would create a huge burden on me, the author guy, to reproduce.

Should you be so adventurous, and live such a completely useless and boring life, as to want to read this in the native languages, arrangements have been made.

You can order the unstandardized edition through the Nozama Trading Guild. It will be translated and shipped from Solipsismia.

Solipsismia Books takes pride in providing the highest quality translation in the known galaxy covering nearly one million language variations.

Helrisien translations are not guaranteed.

Solipsismia Books takes no responsibility for accidentally insulting your parentage.

The Pirates! adventures are dedicated to the most amazing woman in the galaxy.

Agnes… I miss you with every word I mispell, and every, comma, I misplace.

Galactic Standard Common Exclamations

In order to ensure smooth communications among the many civilizations that blanket the galaxy, a standardized set of exclamations was established by the Post Hypocrite Language Update Research Group (P.H.L.U.R.G.). Thereby making it possible for anyone to understand if someone is hurt, angry, insulting or just frustrated during communications.

To none of the other civilizations' surprise, the Earth refused to ratify this and several other agreements. Calling them 'senseless pandering to liberal elitists'.

Phlurg – Excrement. Usage is equivalent to Earth English term 'shit'.

Phall – The rough equivalent of where the 'faithful' think you go when you die and you've been a very bad person, or a politician.

Nearest Earth English term would be 'hell'.

Hasblath – A really dumb six-legged bovine creature. We're talking stare at the sun dumb. Often used in expressions of insult or contempt, 'hasblath brained'.

Meat makes excellent jerky.

Grak – Similar to Phall in that one would be 'graked to phall'. Nearest Earth English term would be 'damn'.

Frigid – Modern galactic standard replacement for ancient expression 'cool'.

Cool still used on Earth for some reason.

Fishile – A common expression of frustration or exasperation with no real meaning.

Pronounced as if someone in a food shop were telling you where you can find the salmon.

Filjab – The slang word used to describe a common sexual act; a case where something is completely broken (filjabed); to insult someone (you filjaber); to tell someone to go away (filjab-off); you get the idea.

Farlaph Phlurg – The excrement of the Farlaph Beast. A particularly disgusting creature whose odors are so repugnant they cause humanoids to pass out cold. You can well imagine, their phlurg is no fun to step in.

Introduction

Through this series of books, you will have the opportunity to experience adventures that, in the distant future, will shape the history of the galaxy.

Some thousands of stanyears from your now, some hapless hero will find a copy of this series of books in the ruins of some post-apocalyptic Earth library. After being chased by zombies, vampires, zombie vampires... whatever... that hero will read them and realize, to their horror, that all of this could have been prevented.

In a moment of heroic delusion, they will invent time travel to go back in time and change the past that leads to this future preventing this present from happening. Of course, by then, this present will be their past which created their present in its future. Forget all that.

For once, just use your present to prevent your past from becoming your future.

– One –

The galactic cruiser is blasting away from the planet Elttaes under full power. Gaining too fast for comfort is a large swarm of attack drones from the Nozama Trading Guild. Their weapons firing repeated pulse cannon volleys against their prey's shields. The shields are shimmering with splashes of rainbow colored energy from the blasts. The automated gun turrets on the cruiser are returning fire. With all the evasive maneuvers the drones are performing, the effort is as futile as trying to swat flies in-flight.

The cruiser is impressive, but by current galactic standards, not huge. Its surface covered with weapons systems of incredible variety. Visible cannon turrets outnumbered by a multitude of hidden turrets and torpedo bays.

Its most outstanding characteristic is that its surface appears to be a shimmering royal purple liquid, because it is. It's composed of an advanced form of liquid-composite with the ability morph the ship into any form. It's also possible to rearrange the interior as well. Giving it the ability to provide many more, and much larger, interior compartments than appear possible.

Along the leading edges of the ship are the only markings. In space-glo safety yellow the words *Thrill of Agony* are bracketed by markings that bear a resemblance to a skull and crossed bones. A resemblance due to the fact that a skull and crossed bones is exactly what the markings are. Beneath these markings is a scrolling signboard that reads 'On Sens-O-Cast Now... STAR WARS... EPISODE MMCMLVI... JEDI MASTER CHEFS...'

In the warm pastel glow of the bridge, the only obvious crewmember reclines in a control couch. He's a young, muscular, some would say attractive but otherwise an ordinary looking humanoid. Seriously, he's cute but nothing to get all aquiver over.

His Dial-Your-Style activity suit is form fitting with flared cuffs and tapered legs. A deep and vibrant purple with a muted jacquard stitch. Finished with bright gold buttons and space-glo safety yellow piping, sash and belt. The latest in galactic pirate fashion.

His gaze is laser focused on the holoskin screens overhead. His face is expressionless as he assess the situation. He's pressing buttons and turning knobs with that excited passion people get when they're being chased by things that shoot at them. The buttons and knobs appear to do nothing useful because, well, they don't.

"IRRIT-8! Give me avoidance protocol corkscrew, NOW!" Guy command orders.

The ship begins to spin in a helical pattern. Pulse cannon bolts are now missing much more often. The drones are starting to swirl in the ships wake, some rotating with the *Thrill of Agony* and some rotating counter. Which leads to a number of drone-on-drone collisions.

"That's so filjabing frigid to watch," Guy command laughs.

"CAVIT-8. What's our status."

"EVAC U8! You dullard. We're fifteen stanseconds from the Hyperspace Fly approach limit. It's time to pick a star system to dial Guy."

Guy gives up in frustration and just punches in a random dialing sequence on the Fly Control. He just can't resist one last act of defiance. He immerses his hands in the liquid configuration control pads and concentrates on his favorite rude hand gesture.

As the ship morphs into the desired form, there's a slight lag in the shield's ability to compensate. A lucky blast from an attack drone punches a gaping hole in the main cargo bay. Crates, barrels, garbage and cargo of all description begin pouring out into space.

"Guy! You know shields are less effective during a morph!"

"I know... I know..." using his command sullen voice.

The, now less sleek, purple cruiser slices out of the fabric of hyperspace into a new star system with a scream that, even had someone been there to hear it, makes no sound. The ships antimatter reactor working tirelessly, just as though it didn't matter. The flight pattern is now a degrading and erratic helix, smoke trailing from the port side.

"THING U8! What shape are we in?"

"Guy! How many times are you going to do that? It's EVAC U8! E V A C U 8! And we're in the shape of a rude hand gesture. Middle finger extended."

"OK, don't blow a bubble RAM pack you pedantic bucket of bits. I know what form we're in. I meant what's the condition of the ship?"

"We have multiple malfunctions ship wide including morphing control, sauna containment, orientation control, sanicube sludge containment and there are some odd readings from the antimatter reactor."

At the point where the ship entered space-standard is an immense opening through which planets of the Elttaes star system are still dimly visible. The attack drones have scattered to return to their base. The opening is closing and appears to be an immense zipper. When a Hyperspace Fly closes, it makes a thunderous *zzzzziiippp* sound, no one has ever heard.

A Hyperspace Fly requires tremendous energy to function. Therefore, they're placed in close proximity to the star, or stars, of star systems. They draw energy directly from the star to fold the fabric of space between two Flies. Although many argue that space is made of plastic, not fabric.

History vids relate that the creators of the Flies, the Sundbackians, are now long gone. They were born on one of the first habitable planets to form when the galaxy was still young. Many argue they were the most advanced race yet to evolve in the galaxy. Earth humanoids take exception to that designation while presenting no clear evidence to support their belief. Nothing new.

The Sundbackians mastered sickness, hunger, energy and interstellar travel. Their society so evolved they no longer required a formal government. They became so technologically advanced that they'd run out of challenges.

To alleviate the boredom, they set out on a project of immense importance to the future of the galaxy. To connect the entire galaxy with the Hyperspace Flies.

The project managed to keep them occupied for a few stancenturies before they ran out of useful galaxy. The disappointment was unbearable for their advanced egos. They surrendered and just stopped evolving or caring about anything.

As the story is told, the disappointment became unbearable. In a final act of depression and desperation, they committed infocastcide. They sealed themselves in total emersion infotainment cubes and died from the exposure to infotainment broadcasts from across the galaxy. A gruesome torturous death that arrived only after their brains turned to jelly.

Guy command groans at the computer, "Hey, ACCENT U8, where are we anyway?"

"I'm currently trying to establish our position in the space time continuum. Or at least a close approximation of where we might be, since we certainly are not where we're supposed to be, or might want to be if we're going to have to be anywhere at all." EVAC U8 is more than a bit perturbed by their situation.

The bridge of the *Thrill of Agony* is the penultimate in control environment design. Holoskin screens float about tracking the crew's movements so they can be at a pleasant height for viewing at any time. All the controls are designed to be user friendly. A 'shake hands with the plasma cannon' style of ergonomics pervades the environment. The ship is capable of providing a large selection of configurations and environments including antique space craft, incredibly intricate modern craft and classic chrome. Also available is a Nouveau-Techno-Artos environment, which most find too confusing. The ship is capable of morphing the interior into almost anything you can imagine.

The command couches themselves are amazing

examples of being engineering. Their overall appearance is that of a humanoid hand anchored at the wrist with fingers stretched upward and back at a slight angle. The 'fingers' wrap around the occupant during high-G acceleration and deceleration providing critical life support and preventing severe physical trauma. The 'thumb' of a couch is a multipurpose control console capable of reconfiguring itself based on user need. The couches can adjust to accommodate any form a being may require; humanoid, bovine, reptilian, you name it.

Scientists and engineers discovered that, with the introduction of the quantum anthropomorphic computers (QAC), starship captains spent much of their time in a reclining position. It was also discovered that they have grak little to do with running the ship.

As a result, the command couches are designed for the ultimate in comfort and entertainment. Controlling the ship is a secondary function. The bulk of the lights, knobs and switches attached to the 'thumb' have no real function. They're only there to help the crew while away the stanhours in a harmless way.

Always consult the manufacturer recommendations and safety warnings before enjoying your couch. Manufacturer is not responsible for death of occupant by the complete compression of all internal organs if operational procedures are not properly followed. Or, really, much of anything that happens to you.

Guy notices that the distant hum of the antimatter reactor has become much more distant. The antimatter now matters.

"What's up with the reactor system EVAC?"

"Antimatter systems have become unstable Guy. Shutdown sequence will begin in seven stan-minutes."

"Great! Now we're going to have to find a place to repair the ship. You know how much I hate strange service stations! Always out of hasblath jerky. Grak restrooms are never clean," he command moans.

"Don't have your typical overly dramatic reaction. I detect technology and, though it's too early to be certain, intelligent life on the planet in orbit five," comes EVAC U8's droll reply.

With the impulse drive systems driven to their fullest damaged capability, the *Thrill of Agony* comes swooping down into the largest city on the planet. They come in wobbling, sputtering and heading straight for what appears to be a parade of some kind. They're coming in a little too low for safety, the parade's safety.

True to their name, the impulse drive systems act on impulse. That impulse being to quit. The *Thrill of Agony* begins sliding and bouncing down the main boulevard. The ship obliterates the participants in the parade leaving a rather bloody smear on the wide boulevard. A parade participant is thrown onto the main viewport, startling Guy. He hits the washer/wiper knob on his control couch with a disgusted grunt.

The ship skids to a stop atop a statue of someone whom someone thought was important in the center of the city square. Various body parts strewn along the hull.

"Reactors are shut down. Morphing control is offline, so we're stuck in this form. Oh, and sanicube sludge containment has just failed."

A large eruption of unspeakable waste launches from the tail of the ship. Leaving a small pond of disgust on the square. This disturbs a number of residents and a flock of multicolored flying creatures with bowel problems.

A crowd begins to gather on the square. Although they're angry, and gagging from the odor, they look more confused than anything else by the disaster that has unfolded before them.

"Hey! You could have put us down in a little more diplomatic location XKAV-8. Now how am I going to get any cooperation? The *Thrill* wipes out their parade and then takes a giant poo in the town square. Going to be real easy making friends now, FILJAB!" Guy command complains.

"I guess I can use those persuasive voice techniques I learned at last year's Piracy for Fun and Profit convention. I swear, there are times…" Guy's ramblings trail off as he heads for the main hatchway.

When the hatch opens, the native atmosphere washes over him and his stomach clenches. He's never gotten used to how badly a planet smells compared to the purified air of the ship.

Elbowing his way to the front of the gathered crowd is a being who's the exact twin of our dauntless pirate captain. Guy steps through the air lock and into the pale green light of day. The crowd carries a gasp through its ranks like wind waves on a wheat field. All eyes fall, one each, on the two of them.

Forcing his way in front of the crowd, he exclaims, "Guy! You hasblath brained, chromosome damaged… I should have let those shoulder hunting pygmies on Epsilon Eleven sacrifice you to their virgins. Where have you been!"

With a heartwarming look of puppy-like affection, Guy responds, "Now don't be mad at me Guy. How was I supposed to know you left the ship with those hotties you were partying with? When you weren't on the bridge, I thought you were still partying in your quarters."

"That was almost a stanweek ago!" comes Guy's angry command admonition.

A rather somber military officer steps into the clearing that has formed around the *Thrill of Agony*.

With a mortician's monotone, he announces, "That large group of ugly and angry Nihilists, whose very existence is still in doubt, that was, as if it mattered, going to wipe us out, seems to have been martyred by this physical manifestation perched upon our, now martyred, statue.

"It is quite possible, though hardly probable, that your arrival saved our people from annihilation. It is clear, however, that you do know how to make an overly dramatic entrance."

"Ehhh, yeah, that was a... a... marvelous example of my ability to analyze the situation and take appropriate action," comes Guy's nervous command lie.

The short, fat and pompous politician-type native who's been standing in the crowd behind the other Guy now comes forward and begins puffing his cheeks in obvious preparation for a speech.

"As the probable head of our certainly doomed colony of Solipsismia, I will undoubtedly have to welcome you as a savior. At least until more concrete evidence of your existence can be established.

"Do be aware that, whether you exist or not, you are still welcome to inhabit our consciousness and any reality you are currently enjoying. Your arrival at this exact moment may, though I am not certain, be fortuitous for our citizens. However, your choice of parking spots leaves much to be desired."

He sweeps his arm pointing at the carnage on the boulevard. "The group you so completely, and quite grotesquely, eliminated just now was bent on ending our currently shared reality. For that we will, at least momentarily, be grateful. However, being saved from the inevitable is of dubious value given the ebb and flow of consequence.

"Director Mamang, at your service," he concludes, hand extended in greeting.

Guy is now more confused than usual. Running from the Guild only to find himself crashed on a planet of Reality Analysts then finding his lost brother has taken all the ability to react his body can muster.

He half stumbles as he walks down the ramp and up to where Guy and the politician are standing. He grabs the Director's elbow and wobbles it from side to side in the official galactic pirate greeting.

"I'll be pleased to be your savior. Ahh... assuming we can arrange a little minor repair for my, uh, our starship." Guy is using his persuasive voice techniques.

"Do you normally speak so fast or do you have time lag from your journey?" The politician looks confused.

"Oh well, it does not really matter as the stress of this day may well be creating this illusory reality. You may end up not actually contributing to our perceived existence in the final analysis. All of this is too random for us to assign probability with any certainty," he reassures.

"I don't mean to stick my nose in your business, whatever that is, but isn't that a bit of a bad attitude?" Guy asks.

A gleam, if someone so overtly boring is capable of a gleam, comes to Director Mamang's rather pale gray eyes as he answers. "I suppose, in the short-term appearance of the physical manifestations you accept as reality, my statement might seem a little counterproductive.

"However, if one sees the entire picture with our clarity, it becomes apparent that this is simply not a permanent conceptualization. Having any attitude, good or bad, simply does not alter the possibilities we will be presented."

"Oh," is all Guy can say.

"In any case," continues the solipsist, "we will be happy, although that is a most transient state of mind, to assist in the repair of your craft," he concludes.

The Guys and the Director head off to make arrangements for the repairs.

"Captain Jak here can arrange everything you need," says the Director, pointing to the officer who first addressed him when he, well, landed.

"Let's get to work!" comes Guy's command greeting as he slaps Jak on the back.

Then the Guys exchange a thought, *And hit the first mood elevation station we can find!*

The Guys are not just identical twins with identical names. Their father was an Earth humanoid telepath. And more than a little odd. This resulted in the Guys inheriting a handy characteristic. Along with their half-witted approach to life.

Their father's genes bequeathed them the ability to exchange their thoughts. They can't share or read each other's thoughts in real-time. For the Guys, only one of them can have the thought at any one moment in time. In order for Guy to know what Guy is thinking, Guy has to forget about the thought entirely.

This phenomenon has led many evolutionary psychologists to speculate that everything a person remembers has already been forgotten.

As they walk away, the scrolling sign board on the bow of the *Thrill of Agony* now reads 'OUCH!!' in blinking red letters.

◊ ◊

The Solipsismian tech team gets to work, under the direction of EVAC U8, repairing the various damaged systems on the *Thrill of Agony*. The Guys find a mood elevation station and settle in to catch up, and catch a buzz.

"How'd you end up trapped here among the reality confused Guy?"

"After you left me stranded on Xelent with the hermaphroditic pleasure hunters, I was taken captive. OK, it wasn't a hard thing for them to take me captive. After twenty stanhours of wild sex and mood elevation, I was already a captive. What I didn't know was that they intended to keep me as a pleasure slave. Guess I made a good first impression." He smiles a wry smile.

"By the time I found two working brain cells, they had me on their ship. We were boosting off of Xelent and traveling to their next planned orgy. Before we made it far, a cruiser from the Xelent authorities swooped in on the ship and demanded they surrender. The captain hit overdrive and tried to run for it. So, naturally, we were attacked by the cruiser.

"Apparently, the pleasure hunters have a nasty habit of holding wild orgies, robbing the participants, kidnapping a few and then boosting while everyone is passed out from all the fun. Worked on me. I guess the authorities got called in faster than they expected.

"We took a lot of damage and were almost out of hope. The pleasure hunters were blasting toward the nearby Fly. It had barely unzipped when we passed through in a hail of cannon fire. Pretty frigid and exciting. Given I survived, that is.

"Anyway, we blasted out of the Fly on this side damaged and pretty much out of control. The Xelent cruiser was hot on our tails. The usual silly space chase stuff was happening everywhere; sparks flying, lights blinking on and off, odd unexplainable little explosions along the corridors, people running down the corridors screaming for no obvious reason, steam venting from saunas, sex toys flying around and rolling along the corridors.

"It was total chaos on the ship so I made a run for an escape pod. Had to dodge all the crap flying around, almost lost it when I rounded a corner and hit a minefield of vibrators rolling all over the corridor. I made it just in time and shot myself out of the ship. The pod's automated systems picked this pile of rock to drop me on.

"Really, kind of too bad when I think about it. I was having a blast until they got all kidnappy about it."

With a cold scornful look, Guy asks, "What the phall took you so long to find me!"

From the look on Guy's face, he's trying to make something up fast. "Well, now, calm down Guy. First of all, you know that the time dilation effect means time for me was different from yours. It's only been two standays for me." He likes that one, it's true-ish.

"And I really wasn't looking all that hard. We always come back together. See, like now. Never fails." He ends with a weak, and hopeful, smile.

"Oh sure, not even looking," Guy glowers. "What were you doing on your standays and what've you done to the *Thrill*? Bringing her in limping and wounded like that!"

Guy gulps and tells his story...

◊ ◊

Guy begins to relate how, when he left Xelent, he headed to Elttaes according to plan.

"HEY! Author guy! What the phall are you doing? This is MY story!"

Oh yes, of course. Please continue.

"Fishile!" with a dismissive cock of his head, "Some authors are so into themselves!

"After we, I mean I, left Xelent I headed to Elttaes according to plan. Deliver the cargo of phase shifting diurnal diamonds to the Nozama Trading Guild, pay off our debt and party on."

Guy interjects, "Andakosh takes good care of us. I'm sure he was happy when you delivered on schedule." Guy is being optimistic, or delusional.

Guy continues, "Yeah. Well. Things didn't go so smoothly on the way to deliver to the Guild. I got distracted and stopped off at the Distraction Station on Elttaes' largest moon. You know the one. You said we should never go there because it's dangerous to play so close to the paycheck. Now I understand why.

"They have the most amazing casinos! Naked pansexual wait staff, full throttle drinks and every form of gambling you can imagine. They have a zero-G mood elevation station that's unreal! The lounging couches at the tables even have joysticks! Did I mention the eer weed vending machines? We're talking pleasure in EVERY form."

Guy isn't looking impressed as he hits the feed button on the mood elevator, hard.

"I was doing pretty well at the 3D poker table and getting a good buzz on. I think I was up by about a hundred thousand credits when it started getting hard to keep track.

"That's when this hotter than hot Flipmeendo chick comes up and starts rubbing on me. You know the ones, breasts on the front and back, ahhh. She was beautiful and full of sweet talk. She plied me with several drinks as I chatted her up.

"She told me there was some serious betting going on around the MMA Hockey League playoffs. She convinced me it would be easy credits because she knew a player with an inside line.

"Next thing I knew, we were on our way to the sports betting pit. Things started out OK. I made a few thousand credits on the first match. Then my luck decided to go elsewhere." He sighs.

"I guess I never got a good handle on how the most blood thirsty team with the most penalties is the one to bet on. I bet big on the team with actual athletes. So much for that inside line the hottie had.

"They were doing awesome until the other team took the legs off of their goalie. Sliced them right off at the hips. Made a huge bloody mess on the ice, let me tell you.

"By the final period of the match, half the ice was red. The team I bet on was down to putting the water boy on the ice. Most of their team was on stretchers or in body bags. Unbelievable carnage!

"By the time it was all over, the Flipmeendo hottie was nowhere to be found. Guess I should've seen that coming. I lost a lot, I mean a LOT, of credits."

You see, Guy has never really followed galactic sports all that closely. Mixed Martial Arts Hockey gambling isn't for inexperienced sissies. He really should have stuck to 3D poker.

"HEY filjabing author hasblath!"

Oh, yes. You know, it is my job. No need to swear at me. Last time.

"Phlurg! Where was I?

"When I went to try and work something out with the Settler, he wanted our entire cargo or my right arm. I bargained hard and ended up having to surrender half of the diamonds and clear out, which was fine by me. I did manage to keep a decent stash of eer weed though."

"So, half our cargo is gone?" asks Guy.

"Well yes, but I guess you could say it was our half since Andakosh only paid for half up front.

"I'm now heading to the Guild facility on Elttaes all whistling and happy. I didn't lose the entire cargo and I figured Andakosh would be lenient getting the half he'd paid for right away.

"The Settler must have contacted the Guild. I'd just touched down in a bay at the Guild cargo facility when they contacted me. They said they were aware of an issue with the cargo and were claiming the ship as collateral for full delivery due. They gave me the old 'Please Step Away From the Ship' all full of attitude.

"I'd have none of that so I did an emergency burn out of the bay. Did some of damage to a wall and a number of shipping containers. Feel bad about that.

"Faster than I thought possible, they scrambled attack drones to disable and confiscate the *Thrill*. I'm sure Andakosh wasn't trying to destroy us. He's tough but he likes us. He was mad as phall though. The attack and confiscate was just over the top. If you're mad at me now, imagine how mad you'd be if I hadn't even been able to rescue you?"

"Yeah, like rescuing me crossed your mind before you saw me today." Guy stares off in another direction and refuses to make eye contact with Guy.

"Hey, that's harsh Guy. You know we always find each other.

"Now comes the exciting part where I fight my way out of the system."

"Oh, please, do get to the exciting part," comes Guy's command sarcasm.

"The *Thrill* is a fast ship and I was using our hidden secondary impulse boosters. But the Guild drones are much lighter and accelerate really filjabing fast. The ship took a lot of heat on the way to the Fly and I ended up just dialing random numbers to open the Fly right before they would have caught us. Left them scattering to avoid going through the Fly. Good thing attack drones lose their control signal if they pass through a Fly. I ended up here and, as you can see, in pretty rough shape."

"So you're telling me that you lost half the cargo, ripped off the Guild and then damaged our ship just for good measure!" Guy is waving his arms and not using his command happy voice.

"I guess that sums it up. Except for the part where the rest of the cargo was lost."

"UGH!" Guy's arms drop limp at his sides.

"I thought we were in the clear and then an attack drone got in a lucky shot. I'd just configured the *Thrill* to give them a salute on the way through the Fly when they blasted a nasty hole right in the cargo bay. We'd taken so much damage that it took the *Thrill* too long to heal itself. The rest of the Guild shipment, trash and anything not tied down was being sucked out the hole."

Guy rubs his chin slowly. "Oh, I see. So we're out of credits in the public account? We have nothing to sell? And the Guild is looking for us? How lovely." He hits the MAX button on the mood elevator and groans.

Guy is sweating and fidgeting in his couch. You can tell by the pained look on his face that he's searching for a change of subject.

Director Mamang saunters up. "Gentlemen, it would be our sincere pleasure, assuming the future is predictable, to have the two of you join us for a little dinner gathering this evening. It is not often we have visitors and are saved from what may have been certain death on the same day. Assuming anything can be construed as certain."

Guy replies, "We'd be delighted!"

"Perfect. My humble conceptualization of a home at eight then. Looking forward to it!"

Guy thinks, with a look of relief on his face, *Change of subject FOUND!*

Guy adjusts the dials on the mood elevator to fine tune his buzz and tries to forget what he's just heard. Thinking, *We now have no way to pay the Solipsismians for the repairs to the Thrill. We just can't help but make friends wherever we go.*

◊ ◊

That evening, the Guys arrive at the Director's residence for dinner. Voices are loud and someone is banging on a table. They buzz the doorbell.

The director appears at the door. "Hello Guys! Please, accept this conscious construct as my home. Come in, come in."

The house is stately and appears to be a work of love. Fine woodworking and attention to detail are abundant throughout. To one side of the entry hall is a library that's overflowing with books on shelves that extend floor to ceiling.

Guy comments, "Director? Are these real books? Like the ones the Classical Hippies read?"

"Yes, indeed, Guy. These particular books were brought here by the Forbearers many stancenturies ago. Amazing are they not?"

"Yes. But you leave them just lying around?"

"Heavens, yes. We actually read them. The experience is beyond comprehension compared to the holoscroll books. The physical manifestation of words pressed into paper. Not just bits and bytes waiting to disappear and be replaced. You can imagine you are holding reality. The experience is much deeper, much more fulfilling, than you may be used to.

"It is not just Classical Hippies reading actual books anymore. They have made quite a comeback and have become all the rage among the enlightened civilizations of the galaxy. You should try one sometime!"

"Uh... yeah..."

Guy notices one sitting near the door titled 'Reality... What a Concept!' he groans and thinks, *That would be hilarious if it weren't serious*.

As they walk into the dining area, they see four men sitting around a carved wooden table heaped with, well, it must be food. The Guys scan the table and see things that appear to be proteins, a few things that appear to still be growing, several things moving in various dishes and an odd blue-green liquid in decanters being drunk by the group.

To Guy's astonishment, in an ornate urn at the center of the table sits what must be mirage. Guy's mind is racing.

Chocolate covered doughnuts! Filjab! I'm in paradise!

The thought is so intense that it bounces back and forth in his brain for a moment.

The Director says, "Gentlemen, Gentlemen... please! Our guests have arrived. I believe you are all acquainted with one of the Guys? We now have the pleasure of the company of two Guys. Quite a unique manifestation for a life as mundane as ours. Our little moment in pair-a-guys."

Everyone laughs. The Guys just look at each other and moan.

The usual wave of garbled together salutations and greetings from all speaking at once crowds the room.

The Director continues, "You see, we are having rowdy fun debating your existence. Most still think you are a manifestation of a shared hallucination conjured under extreme panic at the approach of the Nihilists army. We created you in our reality to escape an undesirable future reality. Most fun we have had in some time, I dare say."

The Guys are directed to two empty seats and a portly man throws them glasses of that inebriator they're drinking. It is blue-green, effervescent and there's something is swimming in it.

"Here, you will need this!"

Guy takes a deep drink. "WHEW! Now this is tasty and has a real kick to it."

"It is a local distillation that we created to increase the clarity of our debates regarding reality, or the lack thereof. The little creature swimming in the decanter gives off a chemical that is mildly hallucinogenic. Allows one's mind to open up to new possibilities. Oh, and see some great colors," the Director explains and then drains his glass.

"Another!"

Captain Jak speaks up, "So, Guys, you travel the galaxy widely as I understand it? I am curious if you have yet encountered Profits?"

The Guys eye each other and then, in unison, ask, "Profits? You mean as in 'Have we made any credits?' type of profits?"

"No, no," the Captain continues, "the Profits who are a mystical group who have been aggressively, some say militaristically, spreading a new religion in the galaxy. From what I understand, they are based on Earth. Of all places!"

Another in the group chimes in, "Yes, it is true. From what I gather, they have amassed fantastic wealth and moon-size orbiting stations full of office supplies are being spread across the galaxy."

The Guys exchange a thought so hard that their heads sway from the momentum of it leaving one mind and entering the other.

YES! That's the answer! Office supplies are an easy sell to the Guild. We need to go to Earth and do some serious pirating NOW before the Guild finds us.

Captain Jak adds, "My sources say the actual name of this insidious group is the Pan-Man-Poo. Some say they are linked with the black accounting arts. They are organizing and outsourcing planets across the galaxy. Bringing order to the galaxy while slowly taking control.

"These days, we think more disorder would be healthy for the galaxy. So many things have become disconnected from the possibility of various realities. Everything labeled and filed in neat taxonomies.

"News feeds that track your interests, advertisements for products they already know you will buy. Our very thoughts filtered, analyzed and regurgitated in neat packaging. People are manipulated by what they are fed. Secrets no longer kept through the use massive data mining. So much predictability stifles the growth of the mind."

Guy provides a command cover story. "We've had a run in or two with the Profits, as you call them. We prefer to call them the Poo." He chuckles but they don't seem to get the humor.

"They're a nasty bunch to be on the wrong side of. We avoid them every chance we get."

The Director interjects, "Of course, most of us have not yet decided if such a thing as these mystic Profits is possible given our inability to observe their existence or validate the futility of their purpose.

"The very concept that someone can take control of planets and generate obscene revenue when all they are doing is telling them what time it is using their own chrono. Seems despicable. Getting outsized fees for adding very little of real value!"

"Hear, Hear!" from the group.

Captain Jak adds, "Incredible indeed! To take away the limitless possibilities in life for a set of codified actions and reactions. All calculated, charted and optimized for profit. What, I beg you, is the value added in that!"

"Please, everyone, let us not starve our honored

guests any longer. Time to eat!" the Director insists.

The men around the table begin grabbing handfuls of the various slimy and bizarre dishes. Piling their plates high with odd edible things, some of which are still wiggling.

Guy grimaces, *They eat like rabid monkeys.*

Guy reaches for the chocolate covered doughnuts in the ornate urn near him. The Director reaches out with a firm, but gentle hand. "No, my dear boy, those are just decorations. Here, try a handful of par boiled olaffub intestines. A great source of both protein and probiotics. Good for your health!"

Guy's face sinks as though it's melting. All he can think of, or taste, right now is chocolate covered doughnuts. As he tastes a handful of intestines, a thought crosses his mind, slowly so as not to disturb vital organ function.

I wonder if these Solipsismian freaks are on to something. These guts taste like chocolate covered doughnuts!

Guy asks, "So, tell me. How did you come to settle this planet? It's a little off the beaten path."

The Director coughs to clear a chunk of food from his gullet and offers up an explanation. "It all started several stancenturies ago. Our forbearers are all from Earth. Yes, the same one the possibly real, and likely accursed, Profits hail from.

"They, our forbearers, were a large group of metaphysicians, philosophers and deep thinkers of every stripe who believed that reality is a concept to be pondered endlessly. They decided that humanoids had become obsessed with things and status. Making life way too organized and way too shallow. They set out to find a planet to call their own.

Where they would be free to think what they want. To determine the validity of existence, anything's existence. To observe the absurd random disarray of the galaxy and ponder it."

The eating and drinking is getting louder and messier. Some at the table are slurring their words and their wild gesturing shows they're losing control of their limbs. The Director has to raise his voice to continue.

"As the stancenturies passed, those of us here in the Solipsismian camp evolved to the position that we should take control of our reality. They decided that there was nothing wrong with building cities and accepting the existence of basic sanitation, food production and flush toilets. Although the commune life had its advantages, free love being one, there is nothing better than a hot shower.

"Over the generations that followed we engaged in minor interplanetary trade, built a successful book translation industry, built the wonderful city and homes you see today. We're not sure why, but almost no one we trade with ever seems to want to visit us. Most often, we have to go to them to do business. We seldom get invited to stay for dinner.

"The Nihilist group among us found those concepts repulsive and set off into the wilderness to deny that anything, or any of us, have intrinsic value. That life, in and of itself, is meaningless. Why bother with growing a society, having laws or possessions. As the decades passed, we prospered and they devolved into nothing more than wolves.

"Things had come to a head when we expanded our farming operations into new forested areas. The Nihilists believe that when we abandoned living in nature, we abandoned any right to it. A preposterous position to take. They began raiding our work teams and destroying our equipment.

"Today, of all days, they decided to mount a full on attack. We are still debating whether such a thing as fate can exist. I, for one, am on the side of serendipity. You were not meant to arrive and save us. You bounced off of all the possible outcomes and landed, I should say crashed, here. The crushing blow you dealt them settled the argument for a good long while.

"The Nihilists will not have the resources, nor will, to bother us again for some time. Again, for that we are thankful. We could never agree on whether to accept the reality of their attack and were quite unprepared. We have always been a peaceful people. More focused on debating reality than fighting with it. The good Captain Jak here represents almost the entirety of our military capability," he concludes.

"Wall shaid Dirmecter!" Jak tries to slur out an agreement.

"Come now gents, all this story telling kept me from staying up with the drinking. Drink up!" The Director overfills the Guys' glasses and his own.

The evening continues with copious amounts of that inebriator is being consumed. The conversation wrapping in upon itself with debates of reality as a concept, the inevitability of unfortunate events and the futility of trying to know anything but one's self. The Guys are drinking faster and faster. Things are beginning to make more sense to them. A concerning development, if concern were any longer possible for the Guys in their current wasted condition.

A few gents wander off. As the evening closes,

the Guys, Captain Jak and the Director are face down on the food-covered table, passed out cold.

◊ ◊

The next day, from within the *Thrill of Agony*, an angry whining voice. "Don't worry about whether I'm being in two places at once when I'm nowhere at all! We're twins! Just install those antimatter parts as if it might matter!"

Ugh! Why do they want to debate reality with a head that hurts this badly?

Guy returns to the ship to see how things are going. Guy has returned to the bridge and is now checking readouts, reading checkouts and adjusting adjustments.

"Oh, hey Guy! Looks like the ship morphing configuration controls are back on line. I was just about to test them," Guy says, as he moves to another console.

At the configuration controls, Guy immerses his hands into a pair of liquid metallic pads on the console. His hands settle in. "Let's give it a try."

After a few stanseconds, the ship responds to Guy's thoughts of a form. The ship transforms itself from the rude hand gesture configuration into a huge chocolate covered doughnut. In the process, destroying the nearby fountain and a playground in the city park.

When Guy sees this, with a sigh that's a combination of disdain and resignation, he command shames, "Oh fishile... here, let me do it!"

Guy takes over the controls and the ship transforms into its normal form, if there is such a thing as normal around these two. It's now a sleek and quite dangerous looking cruiser. Weapons systems of every description lining the hull. The kind of ship perfect for picking up women at a star port.

"Now that's better. Something fitting of the greatest pirates in all the known systems!"

"Wow! Really? We're the greatest pirates in the known systems?" Guy asks.

"I'll let the director know we're almost ready to go." Guy ignores Guy, rolls his eyes.

He and turns to head out leaving Guy to finish the final details. Guy is much better at this type of thing than he is.

Guy stops and turns back to Guy. "Listen. Don't bring up anything about Earth or Profits. Got It? We're going to boost out of here and go straight there. Load up with more than enough booty to pay off the Guild and have credits to play!" Guy is using his command whisper, and it tickles.

Guy goes back to work. He sets the mood-scape for the control systems to Classic Chrome. He loves all the bright colors, chrome, big knobs and levers. He then adjusts the rearview mirror and runs the *Thrill of Agony* through the standard post-repair re-boot and verifications. From all he can see, things seem to be back online.

"CAT U8? Can you verify status please?"

"EVAC U8! Oh, forget it. Yes, I've run a full diagnostic and all systems are green and clean. Though none of them are the color green. What a confusing phrase. These repairs are acceptable, but I would prefer to do a proper job. I think we should plan a trip to The Circus soon."

"Agreed. First we need to makes things right with the Guild."

Heading out to find Guy, he steps into the main hatchway and down the ramp. He spots a mood elevation station and turns to head that direction thinking, *Guy can wait. One more for the road.*

With only stanmicrons to spare, Guy steps off of the ramp between Guy and the Director. They all pause for a moment of confusion.

"Ah! Director Mamang, how nice to almost bump into you," Guy says, as he thinks, *And I gotta face this without drugs!*

"Indeed, and a beautiful day to live, or die, as if the concept of life and death can be considered in the broader context of what is or is not nice. Would you not agree Mr. Guy?"

Guy interrupts, "Hey Guy, the Director here tells me that they've decided that the *Thrill of Agony* is real. Isn't that great!

"Jak's team says they've done about all they're equipped to do on a ship like the *Thrill*. He says the bill only comes to one million standard credits. Not bad."

Guy groans, "Yeah, not bad."

Sharing the thought, *If we only had the credits in the public account, it would be fine.*

Guy receives the thought and shuffles his feet, looking at the ground to avoid eye contact.

The Director says, "We are happy we could be of assistance. If either our being happy or assisting you is of any real value in your perceived reality.

"I must say, your ship is quite amazing. Much better looking now than when you landed."

Guy gives a head nod to the Director. "Thank you Director. We're proud of her."

"I am curious, though. It seems your ship carries a wide array of armaments. What about your current perceived reality requires this?"

"Oh, I suppose we never mentioned it. We're the greatest pirates in the known galaxy." No ego here.

"Ah, well, at least you make an honest living. Unlike politicians," he laughs.

Then he looks confused. "How odd."

"What?" Guy asks.

"I do not remember that playground being in such a deplorable state. We really should get that corrected."

The scrolling holoskin sign board on the bow of the *Thrill of Agony* changes to read 'Solipsismian Books Translation Services... When accuracy and low cost are critical, bring your translation work to Solipsismia...'

The Director smiles. "Ah, I see you participate in the Ad-Sensie program. It is nice to see that our ads are working."

Guy command lies, "Let me go and get my card so we can settle up. Oh, Guy, can you come look at the final adjustments on the decylindracation system with me? Want to make sure that final bit is right before we settle up on the bill."

A few moments after they enter the ship, Guy reappears in the hatchway. In full-on swashbuckle, he brandishes his plasmascimitar, bows at the waist, and exclaims, "Hate to dine and dash, but after all, we are pirates! It's been real... NO! PLEASE! Don't say it! It MIGHT have been real and it MIGHT have been fun, but I know it hasn't been REAL fun!"

The Director just stares in wide-eyed total confusion.

The *Thrill of Agony* roars to life as the hatch slides shut. The hatch slides open again, a technician is bounced out and rolls up to the Director's feet.

The impulse engine systems act on an impulse and the *Thrill of Agony* is blasted toward the stars.

It makes a sonic boom everyone hears. A trail of blue-green vapors tracing its path through the clouds.

What remains of the once majestic statue is just the two legs standing on the pedestal. The torso and arms are scattered on the ground below and lie sputtering and bubbling in the square. The badly burned head rolls back and forth from the exhaust blast.

"FLATU L8, set a course for Earth," comes Guy's command yawn. "I'm going to chill in my quarters for the transit."

"Earth Guy? We haven't been to the Earth system in long time. Are we going to stop by the shipping company on Ceres as well?"

"Not this trip. This visit is for pirate business not business type business. We're going to raid a Pan-Man-Poo ship."

"Oh, my," EVAC U8 sighs.

Guy heads down the corridor toward his quarters. His stride begins to slow and his face is contorted with incredulousness. Before him, the corridor ahead is twisting to the right and the hatch to his quarters appears to be upside-down.

He continues down the corridor. As he reaches the hatch to his quarters, everything within the cabin is normal and upright. He looks back down the corridor where he can just see a corner of the bridge, it's upside-down now.

He yells at Guy, "GUY! You know I don't think this is funny! Now turn my quarters back around right!"

Guy slips his hands into the liquid control pads for the configuration system. He has the look on his face of a child who loves it when a good practical joke comes together.

"Right away Guy!"

Guy stands in the hatchway, his shoulders drooping as a heavy sigh escapes his lips. He sees the corridor twisting and now it's reversed.

"You're such a funny guy, Guy," he mumbles as he closes the cabin hatch.

– 2 –

On Earth, near the metropolis of Pocatello, is the gleaming complex that makes up the bulk of State-of-the-Art Intragalactic Corporation. Elaborately architected buildings, construction hangers and enormous lifting systems cover over fifty square stankilometers. SAIC fabricates ships from the ordinary to the extraordinary from these massive starship yards, often considered the envy of the galaxy. At least they like to think so.

Mechs of every possible configuration whir about fabricating whatever the designers can imagine. Propulsion systems, weapons systems, spas, S&M dungeons and mood elevation stations are designed, built and deployed with amazing efficiency.

Impossible to miss, standing in stark contrast to any other project in the yards, is an ultrasuede monolith. Constructed of an advanced new alloy and electroplated in a beautiful shade of a non-color no one can actually nail down. Is it brown? No. Is it gray? No, not quite. Green? Maybe... The starkness and enormity of the ship stand in striking contrast to the breathtaking alpine valley it now occupies.

An exploration craft of unprecedented construct. The ship is one and a half stankilometers long and one stankilometer tall. The largest a ship can be and pass through the Hyperspace Flies. It bears an uncanny resemblance to a fashion tote.

The *Portfolio*, the new flagship of the Pangalactic Management Pool. She's the first of a fleet of such ships to be commissioned. Not far away, the second portfolio-class ship is in the final stages of completion.

The Pan-Man-Poo (galactic trademark registered) is the result of quasi-religious status among sentient beings across the known galaxy. A group of savagely ambitious management consultants bent on spreading efficient markets, creative capitalism, pinstripe suits and racquet ball throughout the known galaxy. If all else fails, they earn fees plus expenses. Oh, and then there's that diabolical plan thing.

The Pan-Man-Poo are often referred to as just the 'Poo' by non-believers and cynics across the galaxy. A designation the Pangalactic Management Pool is none too happy with.

How did the Pan-Man-Poo become so powerful? There's a detailed twenty-nine hundred forty-two slide Obscure-Your-Point presentation that gives the full flavor of the story. For now, the short version.

Following the Hypocrite Wars, most sentient beings in the galaxy consider Earth humanoids backward. They saw them as unnecessarily and undeservedly preoccupied with themselves. Way too preoccupied with social and religious radicalism to amount to much. Things on Earth seemed so lame that beings from across the galaxy were just about to mark the Earth as boring on all star charts and move on.

Then they discovered the mystic art of Management Consulting. The magical ability to increase profits without increasing expenses has earned the Consultants of the Pan-Man-Poo the folk title of 'Profits' wherever they travel in the known galaxy. This also earned the Earth a two star listing of 'Safe to land. Clean rest rooms.' on the charts.

The Pan-Man-Poo isn't always loved for a variety of reasons. Not the least of which is arrogance. They never seem to end up owing taxes on any planet where they setup operations. Then there's the radical increase in unemployment that seems to follow them wherever they go.

Yes, profits and productivity do increase. But many see the Pan-Man-Poo as corrosive to society as a whole and a lot of the value they claim seems to be shrouded in opaque accounting methods. The numbers just never quite seem to add up for anyone else the way they do when the Consultants line them up.

Inside an oddly shaped building (*oddly* is a geometric shape which has no discernable number of sides) just off the test flight tarmac, is a cafeteria with a reputation for serving something that tastes not at all like food and drink. At a window seat sits Doctor Piobar and his humble, but not hunchbacked, assistant Doctor Prudence Hortense Dincheimer. Her friends call her PhD to save wear and tear on their tongues.

PhD asks, "Doctor? Why have you invited me to lunch at the shipyards? I can think of many better places to eat."

"I have my reasons," he replies. He glances at the Consultants at the table next to them.

Doctor Piobar is the typical university tenured esoteric chemist. A fat jolly man with a big round belly, a bright red runny nose and bushy white beard. He looks as though he spent a great deal of time listening to 'Why don't you take better care of yourself?' lectures. Lectures he obviously ignored.

PhD is another case altogether. She's a full-figured physicist if ever there was one. The only way you can imagine her at a holoboard full of equations is if the holoboard is on the beach and she's in a string bikini.

Not only can she stand up to the best of the modeling world in her Dial-Your-Style activity suit, Dial-Your-Style flowing blonde hair and matching green crystal pendant, she can also take the Nobel Prize for granted. She holds multiple Doctorate Degrees including; Quanta Sincerity, Parallel Existence, Semifactual Argumentation, Zero-G Fencing and Waveform Massage. For her, the most notable achievement is reaching the status of Disciple of the Sisterhood of Relativity.

The Disciples use their Dial-Your-Style hair and activity suits set to provocative and revealing designs. All are beautiful beyond compare. They dress this way as both a badge of honor and to make a statement.

The Sisterhood is responsible for eliminating the male domination of the art of physics. They take huge pride in neither looking nor acting like a stereotypical physicist. If they were not so hot, it would be a real slap in the face to men. But they are that hot, so the men just nod and smile.

There's a general din in the cafeteria. Plates and glasses clinking and loud conversations as techs from all corners of the galaxy try to decide whether to fight the indigestion or just go ahead and end their lives on the spot.

At the next table sit two Consultants from the

Pan-Man-Poo. The Doctor has a focused look and is making an obvious effort not to be noticed as he leans closer to listen to the consultants discuss the *Portfolio*. Which blocks any other view out the windows.

"I still say the damn thing looks like a purse," says one consultant.

He points toward the Doctor without looking. He's wearing a tailored pinstripe suit. The standard uniform of the Pan-Man-Poo.

"You have no sensibilities Bill!" says the other. "It's an ultrasuede corporate brief, not a purse. The impression it makes will give us instant credibility with the unconsulted inhabitants of the far planets. The Partner considers it the best accessory for that all important ten to four look.

"It makes me shudder to think of all the wasted time and motion going on out there," he points toward the ceiling. "Remember your oath Bill, 'Create a problem, then solve the problem. Profits after tax. Planned Obsolescence. It's all in the timing!'

"We've dedicated our lives to organizing the galaxy Bill, whether they like it or not!"

"I know. All I can say is I hope the Poo has considered the risks of sending a crew of Consultants to conquer unconsulted planets... in a purse."

"Hey, watch it! Pan-Man-Poo! You know The Partner inflicts excruciating punishment upon those caught using that derogatory the cynical use for us!"

"You see," says Piobar, "there's my chance to travel the galaxy in search... ahaa chooo!... of the cure. Because of all that useless government red... ahaa chooo!... tape, the funds for finding a cure for the common cold were misallocated to finding a cure for cold weather! Damn fools in Washington!"

Hearing the sneezing, the Consultants pause and look over their shoulders in disgust.

"Doctor, you don't think a cult of Consultants is going to just take you along. What do they care about sniffles and runny noses?" asks PhD, looking rather confused and amused. "Beside the fact that there's considerable profit in minor diseases."

Whispering like a child planning an adventure, Piobar confides, "Take me along! They have shuttle craft on the *Portfolio* that are starships in themselves. They build them as a scaled-down version of their mother ships. They're complemented with all the critical systems and capabilities to travel the galaxy.

"I plan to stow away on the *Portfolio* and appropriate one in the name of the greater humanoid good. The cure is out there PhD... sniff... I am the man to find it! Sniffle..."

"You're going to steal a Pan-Man-Poo ship!"

"Keep your voice down! No, no my dear. Appropriate one. I fully intend to return it when my quest is complete and the cure is found. I'll return a galactic hero. They won't mind at all by that point."

"You don't intend to tackle this alone? You have trouble finding your classrooms at the beginning of each semester. You don't strike me as galactic adventurer. You'll find your cure and then die with it in the depths of space."

PhD doesn't realize she's being set up. Worst of all, set up by a fat jolly man with a big round belly, bright red runny nose and bushy white beard.

"You're quite correct. That's why you're going with me."

Piobar is applying persuasive voice techniques

he learned from the Mediahype delegation that spoke at last year's Creative Chemistry Symposium 'Turning Chemicals into Cash'.

Realizing she has to think fast, PhD stutters, "But... but... I have an appointment to have my Sens-O-Cube tuned this evening. I haven't treated the leather in my dungeon room in a month!"

"A chemists life can get pretty dull... ahaa chooo!... even when one is on a quest," Piobar continues undaunted. "You know the space stuff, and a full-figured physicist is just the thing for my free time. Consider it your duty to a kind man, I mean Man Kind!"

"Welll..." She hesitates as she tries to come up with a way out.

He presses, "PhD, you owe this too me. After all I've done for your career. Hell, you wouldn't even have a career if it weren't for me."

Piobar is forcing her back against her seat with the power of the voice techniques, and his right hand. His nose dripping on his beard.

"Oh, Doctor. Really? It's THAT important to you?" says the startled PhD.

"As I said, we must hurry if we're to be prepared for lift off." On that note, Piobar begins to rise.

PhD, panicking, gasps, "You did not say we're leaving today!

"We didn't order anything to eat yet."

"How can you eat at a time like this," is all he says as he walks away.

PhD notices the Consultants are staring at her amazing geometry in a less than an academic manner. Incensed, she makes the sacred $E=mc^2$ sign of the Sisterhood of Relativity in the air before her and hurries, with a seductive hip swish, to catch up with the retreating Doctor. To her those consultants are relative, she's on a quest.

The consultants take their time studying her angular motion, not to mention her net assets.

Bill comments, "Man! If that doesn't make you want to learn physics, I don't know what would." He whistles quietly through his teeth.

The first Consultant lowers his voice and leans toward Bill. "You've seen The Partner's four hundred eighty-seven slide deck on his Master Plan. We have to appear benevolent and harmless as we outsource the governments of all the known planets.

"The purse, as you call it, is the perfect cover. It's so nonaggressive that they'll never see our conquest of the known galaxy swallowing them whole until it's too late. We will rule the galaxy with quarterly reviewed and detail planned perfection!

"You and I, our options will make us rich. We'll take them as deferred compensation to a shell corporation on Mars and beat the taxes. It's a Consultant's dream come true!"

◊ ◊

Standing in the shadows on the edge of the tarmac between the buildings and the *Portfolio* are Doctor Piobar and PhD. The Doctor is now wearing an ill-fitting black pinstripe suit as a disguise.

"We'll get aboard the *Portfolio* while everyone is at the launching party," checking his chrono. "The Partner is here for the launch and should be on his last few slides about now. He's a master of timing and a psycho about schedules." Piobar is again whispering like a child and looking around anxiously.

What's up with Piobar and the childish whisper voice?

"Don't they have guards? And how do you know where to go?" she asks.

Piobar produces a holoscroll of detailed schematics for the *Portfolio*.

"Yes, they have guards." Pointing down at the holoscroll. "I have that covered."

That answered PhD's questions. She dials her Dial-Your-Style activity suit to match the Consultant's favorite business-formal designer style and dials her hair to jet black in a professional and masculine cut. Which still manages to look hot on her.

Piobar then begins crossing the field, commando-style. PhD can do nothing but follow, he has her by the arm.

"Can't we just stroll up?" she asks.

They step up to the guard. Doing their best to appear as though they belong there.

"Halt! Who goes there!" barks the guard.

"We're on an errand for The Partner," answers Piobar, in his best consultant baritone.

"And just what might that be?" queries the guard.

"He's engaged in an argument concerning a passage from his favorite book, 1001 Enhancements to the Administrative Gene Pool. We've been sent to retrieve a copy from the Commander's library."

The Doctor is using the Mediahype persuasive voice. The guard steps aside, entranced and controlled by the voice technique.

As they step into the *Portfolio's* main entry bay, PhD is overwhelmed by the urge to be organized and productive. It then dawns on her that this is the standard simulated productivity environment on any Pan-Man-Poo craft and in their corporate complexes. She relaxes, for a moment she thought she was having a real experience. The Doctor just sneezes.

Piobar leads on as they journey toward the bowels of the giant starship. When Piobar stops to consult his diagram, and his hanky, PhD takes a look into nearby sections.

What she sees throughout the ship is a degree of organization that would have sent any normal humanoid running to the nearest government offices. Hard science section, soft science section, accounting arts, administrative science, even the rest rooms are color and light keyed to provide the utmost in productive environments. Temperature, humidity, sound absorption, everywhere she looks things seem to fit some kind of evil determinism.

Being a physicist of the Sisterhood, this ordered world is the antithesis of her very being. Physics, during this advanced age, is considered an existential mathematical art form, a genre of techno-philosophy. Currently the 'in' art form and doing well on the various variety Sens-O-Casts. The gaming market exploded when 'World of Quark Craft' hit the market.

It seems as though they're getting nowhere in finding the shuttle bay. Piobar is again consulting his, now mucus covered, diagram. PhD is getting nervous.

"So Doctor, where the hell are we?" with a note of despair.

She leans against the hatch frame nearby above which a gently illuminated sign reads 'SHUTTLE BAY'. This fact has escaped Piobar who's still lost in his diagram.

The hatch slides open with a gentle whoosh. A MaintMech glides past them with a tray of tools and disappears around the corner. The hatch remains open long enough for PhD to notice how nicely the crew has arranged the long-range shuttle craft in their launch bays.

"You know, it's just amazing how organized the Consultants can be. You should look in there," pointing toward the now closed hatch, "and see how nicely they've arranged the long-range shuttle craft in their launch bays," she remarks, as she looks over Piobar's shoulder at the diagram.

"Hmm, yes, they're quite efficient," he replies.

"WHAT! Did you just say!" again with that child-like mischief in his voice, and yelling in PhD's ear.

She's not sure she'll hear out of that ear again. She's also not too certain about how voices are sounding these days. She starts to explain, then decides there just is no explanation.

Piobar ignores her and pounds the entry pad trying to open the hatch. He hasn't quite mastered the Just-A-Touch brand entry pad. As the foray rages between a frantic Piobar's fumbling fingers and an entry pad that doesn't respond well to panic, the hatch again opens.

"Bzzz, Beeep," another MaintMech swerves to miss them and floats down the corridor. Through the open hatch he can now see their destination, the shuttles.

He grunts as he enters. "This place is enough to make you want to throw down some trash."

He grabs PhD and heads for the neat rows of gleaming intragalactic safety yellow shuttles. Running in a zig-zag across the shuttle bay, pausing behind several crates of Caveat Caviar, and then stepping up to the open hatchway of a shuttle number twenty-four.

PhD thinks, *Why does he keep running, dragging me by my arm, when we could just walk? And now he's grunting?*

When they enter the shuttle, Piobar feels an environmental Deja' vu. The interior of the shuttle is almost identical to that of the *Portfolio*, even down to the health spa. They head toward the control center.

"First we have to notify the *Portfolio's* control AI that shuttle twenty-four is out of service indefinitely. Then seal the air lock. That will render us safe and hidden."

Doctor Piobar is certainly sounding more and more like a starship captain. They set about locating all the necessary controls and setting all the appropriate settings so they'll be all set.

PhD comments, "I suppose I should begin getting acquainted with the shuttle's flight control and navigation systems."

The shuttles are another fine example of Pan-Man-Poo expertise. Designed to handle planet-to-planet plus ship-to-planet hauling and also serve as a branch office for the Pan-Man-Poo Consultants.

The control center is multipurpose. Containing both the functionality of a traditional bridge and that of a conference center.

Safety is a high priority with the Pan-Man-Poo. Which means that all the controls that serve no function are colored bright red. The psychology behind this being that, when you panic, you try all the red knobs and switches first. If they're useless, what can you hurt?

More than these types of conveniences, there's an air of planning perfection in every aspect. The control center's command couch even includes a replica of the ancient joystick. It has a new purpose these days, which has nothing to do with steering a craft.

"These Consultants are all business. Look at how efficiently the systems are laid out," PhD comments as she stands taking in small bites of the unique visual stimulus.

"Quite exciting is it not? None of the homogenized experience one gets when planet hoping on those immense passenger cruisers.

"Once we slip away from the Consultants, we'll be galactic adventurers in the grand historical sense! We'll be on our own and making history!"

On your own... all alone...

PhD looks about with a puzzled expression. That voice seems to have come from nowhere and everywhere. Piobar is busy examining the various control systems and hasn't noticed PhD's dilemma.

"I believe I'll go and choose a cabin. Would you like to choose first?" asks Piobar.

"No, there will be plenty of time for that during the outward journey. I think I'll stay here and monitor the takeoff on the holoskin screens. Make yourself comfortable Doctor." She's still looking around the cabin for the source of that voice.

"Have you lost something my dear?"

"Uh... No... just getting oriented."

Piobar turns and walks away. PhD slides, with seductive grace, into a control couch. After punching up the exterior view on a nearby holoskin screen, she becomes engrossed in the output from the control couch. It has analyzed her desires and is caressing her with the joystick.

Piobar almost floats down the corridor as he contemplates the upcoming discoveries. The thought of all the sniffling and sneezing in the galaxy makes his head spin and nose run.

I'm going to go down in galactic history! My name will be in the footnotes of thousands of dissertations.

PhD sits staring at the main holoskin screen. The screen appears to be staring back. In just the time since they snuck aboard the shuttle, the bay has filled with technicians scurrying about making final preparations for launch.

Speech must be over. Won't be long now.

It feels like only stanminutes have passed since they came aboard, because it has been, and now the *Portfolio* is moments from deplaneting.

Deplaneting is like deplaning except that with deplaning you exit one level of reality for another.

There comes a muffled rumble from deep within of the ship. A moment of gravitational disorientation later the *Portfolio* lifts off, rising toward the unknown.

PhD thinks aloud, "The glory of the Pan-Man-Poo realized. A quest begun."

Like most protagonists, she doesn't yet realize how wrong she is in the first and how right in the second.

◊ ◊

The headquarters of the Pan-Man-Poo is nestled in a valley along the coast of what's left of mainland California. California now being a collection of islands and a megalopolis of endless city from north to south along the mountainous coast. The HQ is a 24/7 buzz of activity.

Sleek translucent towers stand boring against the beautiful sky. Each color-coded to its function to aid in rapid identification of the building you're seeking. Otherwise, they're just big boring boxes.

Architecture, to the Pan-Man-Poo, is about function not form.

Flashing across the transparent holoskin surfaces of the buildings are images of attractive professionals looking excited about their work. Motivational and inspiration messages encourage with the usual annoying crap like 'Fly like an eagle!' and 'No I in team!' ad nauseam.

Electric transport vehicles buzz along glass smooth roadways bordered by artificial landscaping. Boring and drab landscaping at that. Nothing of any bright color and all in perfect rows. Artificial provides the maximum in value at the lowest maintenance cost. They practice what they preach.

Given the galactic nature of their business, Consultants work around the clock in shifts timed to prevent anything resembling a rush-hour or that might create a traffic jam.

Floor after floor of each building is identical except for color coding. Rows of open floorplan seating seem to go on to the horizon. Everything is located based on strict calculations of the number of steps required to reach a particular functional area. The desks are allocated one square stanmeter each. Consultants don't believe in wasting corporate space on personal space.

As usual, those in upper management roles are allocated much larger and nicer space. The size and elegance of which seems to bear no identifiable relationship to the amount of the work they do. In fact, if there is a relationship it would be inverse.

In the beginning, the Pan-Man-Poo was controlled by a group of top Consultants who'd been so successful they were granted Partner status. As the years passed, one particular Partner decided that the committee nature of this management structure was slowing down their conquest of the galaxy. His name is Carlos Vadovas and he is, everyone agrees, the most powerful and respected of all Consultants throughout history. His successes as a Consultant are legend. Some say it's he who earned the Pan-Man-Poo the honorific of 'Profits'. His ruthlessness and drive are unmatched.

To affect his management takeover, Vadovas arranged an offsite skiing and planning retreat for all the Partners. He selected a chalet in the Swiss Alps that was nestled against the mountains overlooking a fantastic alpine valley. He didn't travel there along with the other Partners and, what a surprise, there was a terrible accident.

The side of the mountain above the chalet collapsed and crushed the chalet. Burying the entirety of the Pan-Man-Poo executive leadership alive. All save one, who was just landing at the airport. The news feeds reported it as a miracle he wasn't killed with the rest of the team.

After a respectful period of mourning, the deaths were ruled accidental and Vadovas declared himself 'The Partner'. A move that reduced management overhead, streamlined decision making and eliminated tie votes. He's a model of efficiency for the Consultants to worship.

His cut is toned athletic. Tall, but not too tall. Wide shoulders, but not too wide. His face is strong, chiseled and masculine beyond what one would expect from such a boring group of people. He could easily be a Sensie star or fashion model. His hair and suit are selected from the top-of-the-line Dial-Your-Style, giving him the ability to transform his look for every type of interaction.

Today, The Partner is standing just a little taller and a little prouder than usual on a podium at the SAIC shipyards. He's traveled to the launching ceremonies for the *Portfolio*. His face is glowing both from pride in his accomplishment and the excitement of how close he is to executing his greatest plan.

His detailed six hundred thirty-six slide Obscure-Your-Point presentation has received a standing ovation. Charts, graphs, endless bullet points showing how the Pan-Man-Poo is making the galaxy a better place, at a fair profit.

His passion on the podium is infectious to the thousand-plus crew gathered in Pocatello and hundreds of thousands of Consultants watching on the closed-circuit Sense-O-Cast around the galaxy.

A strategically placed spotlight follows his every move as he makes his closing statement. "As we embark on this shining new era in the dissemination of management excellence, the Portfolio Class ships will give us instant credibility. We have designed and built the most complete corporate consulting complex in the galaxy. And it is capable of traveling the galaxy.

"No longer will we have to work through real estate agreements and onerous leases on the worlds we help. Our system-wide headquarters will be orbiting the planets we serve providing critical around-the-clock support to the teams on the ground. Our reach has, now, exceeded our grasp!"

The applause are deafening.

The crew embarks and the *Portfolio* prepares for lift off. The Partner boards his private ship to return to his office. His private ship is a marvel of luxury and efficiency. The entire ceiling of the main cabin is phase change aluminum imbedded holoskin that provides any view and lighting scenario desired. It's set to provide a virtual reality view of the launch.

As he flies away from Pocatello, he savors the view of the *Portfolio* rising from the mountain valley and thrusting into space. The feeling is close to orgasmic.

"The final phase has begun. That speech will keep everyone fooled just long enough." He laughs an evil laugh as the *Portfolio* disappears into the clouds.

◊ ◊

"You may attempt to command the ship whenever you're ready," announces EVAC U8.

Guy opens his eyes and a vast array of impressions strike his awareness. Those impressions, to his surprise, are his view of the bridge. A view which includes several thousand flashing lights and waving waveform monitors. He waves and flashes back. He's noticed the flashbacks a lot since that night in the Acturian Prii Bar, the night he took the orange megadot special.

"Hey CALCU L8, where the filjab are we?" Guy moans. Not sure he wanted an answer, or had even asked the question.

"Please! How many times... It is EVAC U8 oh barely sentient one."

The waveform monitors stop waving and start making rude gestures.

"We're now approaching Earth."

A 3D view of the planet appears on one of the convenient holoskin screens.

Back in his quarters, Guy is also becoming aware of his environment. He looks around, sees nothing familiar, decides to open his eyes, and still sees nothing familiar. Not an uncommon way for this Guy to start his day.

Guy comes through the hatchway onto the bridge, shakes his head, or at least he thinks he might have, looks at Guy with a slightly twisted expression and says, "Hey Guy, what's up or... out or well..."

A klaxon sounds and a convenient holoskin screen comes alive. EVAC U8 simulates a scream, "Craft launch detected! Possible target tracking!"

Both Guys jump into the other's arms. A feat not easily accomplished in three dimensional space.

Dropping each other to the floor, both Guys yell, "Don't do that you pedantic bucket of bits! You scared him half to death with that scream!"

Scraping himself off the bridge floor, Guy grumbles, "Looks like a purse to me."

Guy studies the ship on the main holoskin screen. "Looks more like a ladies fashion tote to me Guy. We should get a reading on their cargo soon. That's if LEVIT-8 here can get around to it."

"EVAC U8... EVAC U8... you dim wits!"

"What did he say Guy?"

"I said I will begin a survey of the approaching starship immediately, if not sooner, sir." EVAC U8 knows when he's dealing with null products.

Guy, now standing for the second time today, makes his way to the control couches. He does love the excitement of taking a ship.

Guy is studying various screens. He's certain the screens are studying him and he's trying to catch them at it.

"Hey Guy, slide over to the scanner station and get us locked in on some of the Profit's goodies."

Guy flashes his fastest glance back at the screens, but they're too quick for him this time.

While Guy pours over scans of the *Portfolio*, and pornie feeds, Guy sets to work checking the tranquilizer torpedoes in preparation for the swashing of buckles, raping of wenches, pillaging and other assorted pirate nastiness fun. Most of which is just in Sense-O-Dramas and his vivid imagination.

They almost never have to swash anyone's buckle and they never rape or pillage. Although they do seem to find their share of pirate nastiness wherever they go.

EVAC U8 updates them, "The survey of target vessel is complete. The vessel is a new design. I'd say more in the shape of a designer corporate brief, not a purse. An exploration craft has highest probability.

"Its automated transponder identifies it as the *Portfolio* of the Pan-Man-Poo. It's carrying a large complement of long range shuttle craft, regular ships stores for one thousand, stanmegatons of Brie cheese, caviar, an unbelievable inventory of useless productivity toys and trinkets plus an incalculable inventory of office supplies. Inventory and locations should be on your screens now."

Guy strikes a piratey pose and belches out orders, "Prepare for boarding! We'll lock on to one of the shuttle bays to get a clear path in and out for the LoadMechs."

Guy loves it when Guy belches out orders like that. Guy tends to like anything that belches.

Guy is tracking the *Thrill of Agony*'s progress toward contact with the approaching Pan-Man-Poo ship. He notices that his crystal necklace is getting warm.

"Should I say something to Guy?" he thinks aloud.

"What did you say Guy?" asks Guy, looking around at Guy.

"I was wondering whether to say something," Guy replies.

"But you just did say something." Both he and the screens looked puzzled.

Guy gets that eerie 'someone is looking over my shoulder' feeling and wheels around to catch the screens. They've already looked the other way, too fast for him again.

"I was going to say how weird it is that my crystal is warm. Is yours?" Guy is watching the screens watch Guy.

"Hmm, I suppose it is. Odd."

Odd… maybe not so odd…

Guy hears a voice from nowhere, and everywhere.

"What did you say Guy?"

"OH PHALL! We're not going through that again. I didn't say anything. Now get back to work!"

Guy goes back to the controls. A small bead of sweat breaking on his brow as he studies the tactical readouts provided by EVAC U8. He can't help thinking about the size of the purse and quantity of cargo. He smiles as he calculates the profit from a haul this size.

A bead of sweat is breaking on the monitor screens as EVAC U8 works to calculate possible attack paths, escape paths and velocities.

Guy leans back in the control couch with an air of supremacy. He inserts his hands into the liquid form configuration pads and the *Thrill of Agony* morphs into the form of a GPS Delivery Ship.

"OK DISIP-8, time to head in. The *Portfolio* has to pass close to the sun to use the Hyperspace Fly. The radiation interference will mask our approach.

"That baby is a sitting duck. In this form, they won't even realize we're pirates until it's too late! Just another delivery… HA!"

The soft mauve glow of the shields becomes evident in the forward view ports. Guy knows that the forward cannons will soon fire with deadly precision into the antimatter pods of the purse. A blow designed to both disable it and render it impossible for anyone to sell the craft as gently used.

EVAC U8 makes final calculations and begins firing. The forward cannons will alternate between plasma and pulse cannons until they've overloaded the *Portfolio's* shield generators and punched holes in its antimatter pods, which look like a lot like the straps on a purse.

In what seems like only a few stanseconds, and is, the *Portfolio* is in trouble. The ship shudders under the impact of billions and billions of accelerated particles. Guy is sweating as he watches EVAC U8 expertly guide the assault. The screens start sweating as they watch Guy.

Blasts of hyperactive particles playing a beautiful spectrum of colors across the view screens. Guy puts on his shades, leans back in the couch and lights an eer weed cigarette.

He thinks, Just can't get enough of watching Guy and the thing with the funny name and flashing lights take out a ship.

Tirelessly prefect, EVAC U8 presses the attack. In no time at all, the *Portfolio's* antimatter drive begins to matter.

"It won't be long now Guy." Guy has an intensity

in his voice that makes Guy tremble with anticipation. Or is it the vibrating massage option on his couch?

EVAC U8 interrupts, "Our attack was a bit overzealous. Instead of just disabling the reactors, the antimatter pods have gone critical. They should be jettisoning them at any moment."

"OK PERFOR-8, open up a channel to the purse commander. Guy, do you think you can handle the tranquilizer torpedo?" Guy never seems to trust Guy.

"Sure thing Guy, but don't you think we should finish up here before we start to party?"

"Not for us, for the Profits, space cadet!" He rolls his eyes and shakes his head.

◊ ◊

In the control center of shuttle twenty-four, PhD wonders, *Now that's odd. My crystal pendant feels so warm against my bosom.*

More worrisome, why is this terminal showing the Portfolio at battle stations and full alert?

"Holy particle beam accelerators! We're being attacked!" She freezes with the words dangling from the tip of her tongue.

She wipes the words away with a trembling hand and heads down the corridor to the crew quarters. In her haste to find Piobar, she flies through a hatchway and crashes into the Doctor as he's exiting a sanicube and zipping his pants.

"Uumff! Good heavens my dear, there will be plenty of time to get physical." Adjusting himself. "You look as though you've just seen the dreaded Crabnorvi. Do try to calm down."

"Calm down!... Calm down!... Sure why not?" Her expression changes from shock to revelation. "I don't have to go on this quest of yours now."

"That's better my dear. Now why don't you hop into the sauna and I'll join you shortly," Piobar comforts her, his expression alternating between consoling grandfather and lecherous old fart.

PhD turns to go. "I'm not sure the sauna is appropriate at a time like this. But I could use some relaxation after a day this weird. Why not."

Hmmm, I wonder if the Doctor should have his hearing checked.

With a complete loss of facial control, Piobar finally absorbs what PhD has just said.

He barks out, "What the hell did you just say! No, I heard you, what do you mean you don't have to go?"

PhD is startled. *Did he just bark?*

◊ ◊

The control center of the *Portfolio* is semicircular in shape with holoskin screens and a vast array of advanced control systems covering walls and ceiling. Everything but the floor is littered with screens, blinking lights and controls. The main viewports extend around the entire bend of the bow of the ship.

In the beams of strategically placed spotlights stands the *Portfolio's* Commander. A tall, silver blonde and athletic man with an air about him that keeps even his closest friends at five paces. In the last stanminutes, that air has begun to thin.

"Why are we being attacked by the GPS? This makes no sense! Didn't we outsource them?"

Ever since they detected the intruder ship, the ledgers haven't been balancing in the Consultant's favor.

"Battle Stations!" the Commander orders in his

command booming voice. "Where are my shields? I need a meeting and a presentation on what's happening ASAP!"

In what seems like only a moment, and in fact is, the battle stations klaxon goes from a call to battle to a death knell.

The grand and glorious expansion of the Pan-Man-Poo may be off for a quarter or two. He thinks, panic in his eyes.

A boiling cloud of steam (sauna on every level) is shooting like a cannon from a ruptured pipe above the shield controls. Sparks are flying as the shield circuitry shorts out. Waveform monitors are no longer waving. The controls are beginning to look more and more like Nouveau-Techno-Artos and less and less like anything useful.

"Get someone from damage control on that console or we'll file Chapter 13 on this one!" Like the distant roll of thunder comes the powerful command voice. Like a dull mumble comes the echo from the empty control center.

As he scans the room for a crewmember, any crewmember, he notices a holoskin view of the shuttle bays. A stampede is in progress. The crew has run for the shuttles and escape pods the moment the antimatter pods began to overload.

He also notices that the strategically placed spotlights are no longer tracking his movements. He looks to the right and sees a bright spot on the floor where he was standing a moment earlier. He throws his hands up in disgust and turns back toward the main console.

He almost jumps out of his command three piece suit when the comport bursts to life. A dashing young man in a lovely deep purple activity suit is on the screen. Ok, the dashing part might be a stretch.

Then he hears, "This is Captain Guy! Surrender and prepare to take on boarders."

"But we really are all full up right now, do you have a reservation?" comes the Commander's unsteady reply.

When he receives no response he continues, "I don't suppose diplomacy will have any effect on this rather unhandy situation?"

The Commander watches the comport with the intensity of a death row inmate waiting for the Governor's call.

"I don't care where you got your diploma, your ship is ours now!" comes Guy's powerful command demand voice. All pirate captains have at least one command demand voice for just this situation.

When he hears this, the Commander's powerful command air dissipates and he begins beating his head against the console.

He's moaning, "My options... my promotion... my ship..."

Too late, he realizes that his forehead has been hitting the 'Jettison Antimatter Pods' pad on the console. He panics, presses his neck and calls the Engineering Chief on his subcutaneous comport (no self-respecting Consultant is without one).

"Chief! Did I just dump the antimatter pods?"

There's a noticeable tremble in his voice and his face is the face of a man begging to be lied to.

Through loud static, and the Chief's heavy breathing, the Commander hears a reply more startling than the loud thud he just heard.

"Holy Spread Sheets! I don't know how you knew Commander. We were trying everything we could. I didn't even see the implosion warning! When you jettisoned the pods you saved the ship sir!"

A little shaky still, the Commander asks, "Say Chief, what was that thud sound I just heard?"

"Not certain sir. Can't hear much of anything down here with half the ship shorting out. Oh shit!"

"What!"

"Readings indicate that their attack set off a cascade in the energy cores of the shield generators. They absorbed more energy from the weapons blasts than they could shunt. This could be bad!"

"You mean bad like not even making out of our own star system on our maiden voyage?"

Again, the klaxons burst to life. The screens show that the *Portfolio* has been hulled. Readouts show the breach in environmental control.

"IT CAN'T GET ANY WORSE!" the Commander is screaming, steam rising from his brow.

He notices a pale blue haze drifting from the ventilators.

"Now that's not good." He drops to the floor.

The strategically placed spotlights start working again and are tracking his head on the way down. He lay face down and prone, illuminated in a pale blue halo of foggy light.

◊ ◊

PhD and Piobar have made their way back to the shuttle control center and are looking out the viewports at the shuttle bay.

Each shuttle is aligned with an individual launch bay and an air lock screening system is used to allow each shuttle to take off without evacuating the entire bay. This is precise planning and the Doctors are seeing it in action. At this moment, every living thing aboard the *Portfolio* can be seen scrambling into the shuttles and escape pods.

"They don't hang around to fight do they Doctor?" chuckles PhD.

With a confused revelation, she asks, "Why is the air in the shuttle bay starting to turn blue Doctor?"

Looking up from his feverish formulations at the financial planning and navigation console, Piobar follows her gaze. "I can't be certain, but I'd guess that is dicopiousopioidcarbolic oxygenate. A fast acting type of tranquilizer gas used for trapping and tagging exotic life forms. I can only guess our attackers intend to take the crew alive, probably for slavery."

"Slavery! Not this physicist!" PhD's tone and expression are of both determination to survive and fear. And she shows it so beautifully.

"Not to worry my dear. We'll be safe from the gas in here. Remember, I sealed us from the rest of the *Portfolio* before takeoff.

"Now please relax, I must finish these computations and formulations if we're going to escape and continue our quest." He turns back to the console.

PhD may have looked panicked before but this is her best effort. She's straining and her voice is cracking as she jumps Piobar.

"Continue! You don't expect to keep going in just this shuttle after all of this has gone so wrong, you're mad!"

"A little angry after all this perhaps, but not mad. This shuttle is sufficient for the journey. We'll use the Flies and plan carefully. My figures show we can make it if we're equal to the task." He straightens and turns to check another set of controls.

PhD leans over to see the figures he mentioned.

The Doctor drops his holoscroll on the 'Clear'

pad. "Oh, I'm sorry, I didn't know you wanted to check those. We must hurry, stand by to launch. We'll make a break in the chaos of all the evacuating Consultants and perhaps the raiders won't notice us."

◊ ◊

Aboard the *Thrill of Agony,* Guy is making final preparations for docking with the *Portfolio*.

"We'll lock on to one of their shuttle bays INDIC-8."

EVAC U8 replies, "Any hatch in particular, oh illustrious giver of all that is unintelligible?"

"Give me a view of the area." And there it is on one of the convenient holoskin screens. "Let's see… okay, take us to number twenty-four."

EVAC U8 brings the ship into contact with bay twenty-four.

"OK, configure the ship for maximum cargo space and open their outer hatch. We're heading for the cargo hold!" Guy command orders as he and Guy leave the bridge.

PhD is in a control couch enjoying the joystick. Piobar is bent over the navigation console. They make ready to escape.

"We will have to be clear of the *Portfolio* before I can connect with the Fly. Open the bay hatch and hold on."

PhD taps the necessary controls and the hatch begins to open.

EVAC U8 didn't register how odd it was that at the moment he ordered the *Portfolio's* computer to open the hatch it opened. This wouldn't have been strange had the *Portfolio's* computer responded to EVAC U8. But it hadn't. At any rate, the hatch is open and that's all he's required to do. EVAC U8 has satisfied parameters. He then opens the *Thrill of Agony's* cargo hatch and awaits further orders.

Piobar didn't look up from his console long enough to note the Collision Eminent warning flashing.

PhD is enjoying the joystick too much to care. Anyway, the arguments with the Doctor haven't been going her way lately.

"Just a malfunction I guess," she thinks aloud.

"What did you say about a malfunction?" asks Piobar, as he stoops over the console, his post-nasal dripping.

PhD responds, "We have a collision warning. Probably just a malfunction caused by the battle."

Just as he's about to agree with her, the shuttle ends its maiden voyage crammed against the bulkheads of the *Thrill of Agony's* forward cargo bay. The ensuing jolt throws PhD into Piobar and they land in a heap on the deck.

Having PhD break his fall isn't at all distasteful to Piobar. Nonetheless, he feels compelled to discover the cause of this latest complication.

"Quick! Get me a damage reading and see what the hell we hit!" he barks, then he pulls his face from between PhD's breasts.

PhD thinks, *Now he's barking again. What's up with people's voices?*

Long before Piobar knows what's happened, EVAC U8 has assessed the situation. He decides to seal the bay and send SpiffyMechs to clean up the area. The *Thrill of Agony* automatically goes to work restoring a workable form in the area damaged by the shuttle.

Guy digs himself out of a pile of broken containers of Viscean antimatter lubricant.

"What the filjab is going on ACT U8? Are we totaled?" he asks.

He clutches the comport controls in a vain attempt to keep his footing.

He thinks, I'm beginning to have real doubts about the whole pirate business. Adventures just don't seem to come out for us the way they do for the swashbucklers of the Sens-O-Dramas.

He slip/slides toward the forward cargo bay while Guy is lying in a pool of lubricant. He looks as confused as usual. He tries to stand, falls forward and slides between Guy's legs and up to the hatch.

"I'll have to remember this stuff the next time we have Guests. What this stuff could do for a game of Testosterone Tag." Guy smiles like an inspired idiot at the possibilities.

"Are you just going to sit there in a pool of goo? Get up and let's see what's happened in the cargo bay." Guy steps down toward the access hatch with a look of contempt shot in Guy's direction.

EVAC U8 blares out a warning, "We've been dislodged from the captive vessel by the impact in the cargo bay. Our assault seems to have set off cascading systems failures and malfunctions across their ship. A shield inversion is imminent. Recommend we put distance between us immediately. Orders?"

"Oh Phlurg!" exclaims Guy. "Get us out of here. Park us behind one of the planets in the system while we sort this mess out."

Guy is using his command pissed off voice and thinking, *Great! No cargo to sell and we have to settle with the Guild sooner rather than later!*

The work lights come up in the bay allowing Guy to see the SpiffyMechs whirring about with dustpans and mops doing their usual efficient job. The

Thrill of Agony has reconfigured itself and sealed around the portion of the shuttle that is extruding.

The next thing he realizes is that the shuttle now lodged in the cargo bay looks a lot like the biggest tote bag he's ever seen.

"Looks like someone wasn't enjoying our party Guy," he says, as he grabs a plasmatronic assault weapon from the locker near the hatch.

Guy's face hardens to that of a mercenary cut-throat. He works the hatch touch pad selecting the 'OPEN WITH DETERMINATION' hex.

He barks, "OK Guy, let's pop that puppy open and see who our guests are!"

Guy takes aim at the shuttle's main hatch. He makes several careful calculations, adjusts the power selector and gently squeezes the fire stud. Nothing happens.

He examines the mechanism trying to understand what went wrong, which distracts his attention from the power pack that Guy has been quietly offering to his back. Just as he spins around to ask Guy where the power pack is, it slaps him in the chin.

"One of these standards I'm going to put you out of my misery!" Guy yells, as he straightens his jaw.

He recovers the power pack, slams it into the plasmatronic and again takes aim at the shuttle.

The first bolt of magenta light streaks from the plasmatronic with its characteristic pew sound and blasts the hatch. After several more well-aimed blasts, the hatch finally collapses inward. It's not at all surprising that Piobar is standing on the other side arguing about whether to open the hatch or wait for someone to show up.

As a result, PhD and Piobar are once again

demonstrating the effects of bodies in random motion.

Sitting on the deck with PhD's head on his lap, he groans, "If I live long enough to get into a space port, I'm buying one of those suites the zero-G hockey players wear!

"I'm just going to sit here and wait for the end. If I stand up they'll just knock me down again before they blast me..." Piobar trails off into a mutter and a series of stifled sneezes.

PhD looks up from his lap and wonders aloud, "My, how familiar those two look. Not to mention how alike."

Yessss... Quite familiar... Quite alike...

PhD stiffens as she hears this ethereal announcement from no apparent source. Hearing voices from nowhere is one thing, but the ominous tone is getting to be a bit much.

Guy is standing in the blasted hatchway. Laying it on thick and loving every stansecond of it.

"Show a little respect for the two most daring pirates in the galaxy!"

Piobar lowers his hanky and looks at his captors with a look of total disbelief.

He cries out, "Pirates! You Guys?"

"Well I'll be! If it isn't the good Doctor Piobar. We haven't seen you in ages, get it, ages."

"Very funny Guy. You two derailed decades of research and then just disappeared. What's this pirate business?"

"Hey Guy, look who we have here."

Guy slaps Guy on the elbow to get his attention. His attention, right at the moment, is owned by the crystal pendant dangling from PhD's lovely neck.

"Oh yeah I, I'm... a... WOW! She has a pendant

just like ours Guy. Look at that." He points at PhD's chest.

"You don't have to tell me twice!" He swings his gaze to the general area where the crystal is hanging.

He lifts his gaze. "Wait a stanminute! That's a face I recognize. It's an unexpected pleasure to have you aboard my dear."

Guy is now laying on a second thick coat of pirate savoir faire. He offers a hand, with a flourish, to aid her to her feet.

"Well, Hi Guy! Talk about a random universe." PhD is now using a persuasive voice technique that requires no training seminars and with which women have a natural endowment.

"I thought you were into intragalactic investments?

"What's this pirate routine?

"And you're a twin?"

Guy and Guy stand enraptured by the music of PhD's voice. Piobar stands up and begins to get more than a little perturbed by the snub. It appears as though he gets a sharp pain in his neck.

Just as Guy is about to ask if he's all right, Piobar starts waving his arms and pronounces, "Biochemists? Intragalactic investments? Who are you two really? Someone is going to have to... ahaa chooo!... explain a few things. We are on a quest and this is not a planned port of call."

Guy realizes he's forgetting something, not uncommon. "Hey, where are my manners! We should find more comfortable surroundings for this reunion. Consider yourselves my," looking at the petrified Guy, who's either turning to stone or in love, "our guests. You won't be going anywhere without us now anyway."

"What do you mean!" Piobar exclaims. "As I Said, we are on a quest and this nastiness will not deter us from our mission. We are destined to go down in galactic history as true humanists. With the... ahaa chooo!... cure we can..."

"In case you haven't noticed doctor, your space dinghy is a little dingy and denty right now," interrupts Guy with a command reproach.

Guy turns, takes PhD's arm in his and walks away. "Right this way my dear. Watch your step."

He leads them toward the bridge. Piobar ranting feebly as he runs, slides and runs through the spilled lube to catch up with the retreating trio.

– III –

The Guys and their new guests walk past a large viewport. Over their shoulders the remnants of the *Portfolio* can be seen in the distance. Its antimatter pods are drifting away in a shower of violent explosions. The ship has begun to crumple in a contorted and grotesque way. The attack caused a cyclical plasmatic inversion in the *Portfolio's* shield generators. The shields are now reversed and contracting upon themselves. Crushing the *Portfolio* into a giant crumpled ball of ultrasuede.

When they enter the bridge of the *Thrill of Agony*, EVAC U8 brings a panorama of space to life on the awesome array of displays for the new guests.

PhD looks around the bridge. A look of confusion sweeps across her face. "I may have distorted sensibilities, no I'm sure I do, but your cargo bay is big enough to hold the shuttle. Now this? This bridge is huge. Where are all the crew and how big is your ship anyway?"

Guy grabs a chance to impress PhD and cuts in just as Guy opens his mouth to offer an explanation, "Oh, it's nothing really. We're the only crew. We just like the feel of a huge bridge. Not so cramped and it just looks frigid. The ship has matter compression and transmogrification technology. The inside of the *Thrill of Agony* can be three times the size of the outside. A feature that is handy for pirate work, finding parking spaces and makes our insurance a lot cheaper."

"Watch this!"

Like an excited teenager, Guy immerses his hands in the liquid control pads. The bridge transforms into a nightclub. Neon lights and disco ball included.

"Now watch this screen." He points at a nearby holoskin screen.

Guy sets a screen to full external view. The *Thrill of Agony* changes from a GPS ship form back to its normal sleek and ominous look that the Guys like so well.

"WOW! I'm impressed," sighs PhD.

A sigh that causes Guy, hands still in the configuration controls, to turn the lights down low and soft music starts playing.

"OOOPS," he gasps.

He returns things to normal. Not that there is a normal for the *Thrill of Agony*.

Piobar interrupts the show. "This is all very interesting and impressive. However, as I said, we're on a QUEST! We need to discuss getting that shuttle dislodged from your cargo bay and space worthy." Indignation showing in the strain in his voice.

Ahhh... yes... the Quest...

PhD looks around at the others expecting to see surprise on their faces as the eerie voice once again appears. Yet no one seems to have noticed.

Guy steps over and, in another display of piratey bravado, says, "Doctor, I do sympathize with your situation. Well, actually, I don't. But after all, we are pirates. Not the walk you out the airlock on a plank type, but pirates nonetheless. Your little purse ship is going come in handy for raiding the

Profits' ships. We can't just let you wander away with it on some foolhardy quest."

PhD breathes a seductive sigh of relief thinking, *Whew! Silly quest avoided and a real adventure beginning. What a great day!*

That sigh causes the Guys to lose their concentration and just gaze at PhD.

Piobar continues to insist, "Foolhardy quest! I don't think you realize the enormity of the humanitarian effort I am undertaking. The entire of humanoid existence has been plagued for stanmillennia by running noses, fever and body aches. That's unacceptable in this technologically advanced age! Those fools in Earth's government have misallocated the funds to curing cold weather. What kind of idiocy is that? I know the cure is out there and I intend to find it!" His face is now bright red.

He continues, "I intend to make haste to reach the planet Mucus Prime as soon as the shuttle is space worthy! They have the most advanced research on upper respiratory diseases in the known galaxy. I'll present my research and insist they assist me."

Guy interrupts, with a tone of conciliation, "Now, now Doctor. I don't think our needs are completely at odds with yours. There are many star systems where the Profits have large stores of booty prime for the taking. Perhaps we can work together. We can use yours and the lovely PhD's skills to help us gather enough to cover our debts to the Guild. Along the way, I'm sure we can make Mustache Prime a port of call."

"It's MUCUS Prime!" comes the Doctor's exasperated retort.

"Whatever. The point is the same. I'm not opposed to quid pro quo when the credits are right. Besides, there may be credits to be made on your little cure idea." Guy is full-on piratey and watching PhD in hopes of impressing her.

PhD is looking around for the source of that mysterious voice, ignoring the argument at hand.

"This is NOT about the credits! Have you no sense of humanity? Do you not suffer from the occasional cold? Do you enjoy snot running down your face?" The Doctor is not giving in.

"Honestly... Yes, it is, No, No and NO!" the Guys reply, in unison.

Guy continues, "The credits you so disdain are what pay for this ship, our gambling habits, drugs and sex. I find those much more important that your quest.

"We aren't afflicted by the disease you call the cold. Although we look like you, well not you specifically, we aren't genetically consistent with common humanoids. In all our three hundred stanyears we've had many things. Mostly after wild parties. All cleared up by meds the morning after."

The Doctor begins to continue making his red-faced arguments and then pauses. "What did you say? Three hundred stanyears?"

EVAC U8 announces, "I am detecting Consultant light destroyers searching the star system. They'll discover our presence soon. Advise please."

◊ ◊

The Partner's lair is on the top floor of the tallest of the buildings in the Pan-Man-Poo complex. Situated in the exact center of the Pan-Man-Poo complex. There was no need for all the offices on the top floor, due to his management realignment, so he had the entire floor converted into just one office.

It's massive by any standards. Walls paneled in the finest extinct hardwoods and all hardware and fixtures are PermaShine brand solid brass. No polishing is ever required as the advanced chemical treatment on the surface makes any smudges, finger prints and dirt just disappear. When he arrives each morning it's as if the office has just been built and untouched.

The room is littered with fine works of art from across the galaxy. Paintings, sculptures and some things that seem to be alive along the walls. Exquisite antique furniture with handwoven rugs of incredible intricacy lining the floors. The room feels more like a museum than an office.

The Partner has no more than settled into his leadership couch when the news reaches him. News that all is not proceeding according to his grand plan. His masterpiece, the ultrasuede manifestation of his ruthless desires, made it less than a stanhour into her maiden voyage.

He's just completing a call with the galactic news services regarding the incident. The news services are, this won't be a surprise, all outsourced to the Pan-Man-Poo. He's making certain the services are silenced. One of the Pan-Man-Poo's guiding principles is to control the flow of information. As they see it, no news is better than bad news and no bad news is good news.

Standing in front of The Partner's massive desk is Supreme Commander Cameron of the Pan-Man-Poo fleet. Cameron commands the massive fleet of ships that the Pan-Man-Poo has spread across the galaxy. Merchant and military ships of every imaginable form providing services to the galaxy, taking control and earning fees. He's been updating The Partner on the launch of the *Portfolio*, and its subsequent destruction.

The Partner's calculating steadiness is dissipating as he brings up the long-range scanner images of the *Portfolio* crumpling into a sad little ball of ultrasuede.

"How did this happen? You say it was a Galactic Parcel Service delivery ship that attacked us? This is absurd!" he rattles off as the Commander cowers in his, now damp, tailored pinstriped uniform.

"We've retrieved a copy of one of the last communications the *Portfolio* received sir."

The Commander hits a few buttons on the holoskin next to The Partner's desk. It replays the images of Guy announcing they're boarding the *Portfolio*.

"Who is this brash, and stupid, young man? Do we have any intel on him?" The Partner wants answers.

"Not much, sir. He shows up in minor criminal and scholastic records but they're scattered across the galaxy. It's almost as if there are two of him.

"I can only assume this was some sort of subterfuge. A stolen ship. The GPS is one of our best clients. They wouldn't be taking such an action,"

The Partner continues, "Have you tracked the ship? I assume you've sent destroyers to intercept and capture them?"

The Commander summons his best command bravado, but it doesn't seem to want to come out of hiding, so he whimpers with authority.

"Yes, sir! We should be getting status at any moment.

"From the last data feeds we received before we lost contact with the *Portfolio*, it appears that one of our shuttles is the only thing that was taken from the ship. The surveillance feed shows a beautiful woman, whom we haven't yet identify, and a fat old man boarding shuttle twenty-four.

"The man is Doctor Piobar, a biochemist. He's been annoying us for some time trying to convince us to help him find a cure for the common cold. He was trying to convince us to take him to Mucus Prime to do research.

"As you may remember, you marked Mucus Prime off-limits due to the plague of upper respiratory illness our first contact party contracted there. We can only assume he was attempting to hijack the shuttle once the *Portfolio* was away from Earth and go there.

"From what we can decipher from the feeds, the attacking ship had attached itself to shuttle bay twenty-four. Piobar apparently tried to run with shuttle twenty-four during the attack, crashing into the attacking GPS ship. It appears he prevented them from achieving whatever their goal was. The attacking ship is probably damaged."

◊ ◊

It's time for our adventurers to beat a retreat. Guy, Guy and PhD are conferring on options, ignoring the Doctor.

PhD snaps to her first piratey idea. "I say we head to the Ulgvar system. The newsfeeds this morning said the Profits have just established a big new presence there. I'm guessing they'll still have huge caches of supplies in orbit around some of the planets."

The Guys look at each other in astonishment.

Simultaneously saying, "Now that's a refreshing bit of realism to hear. Doctor, you should take notes."

The Doctor just frowns. "Harrumph…"

Guy smiles and slides into the control couch. "POSTU L8. Set a course for the Fly at full impulse. Prepare for a rapid transit to the Ulgvar system and set shields to full. Use avoidance protocol long way round."

PhD looks at the Guys and thinks, *I wish I could tell which Guy is on and which is off. How confusing.*

EVAC U8 provides status, "Please make yourselves comfortable in a couch. The G-forces will be intense for this maneuver."

Guy giggles and lights another eer weed cigarette. He slides his hands into the liquid form configuration pads and morphs the *Thrill of Agony* into the form of a wine shipping tanker.

PhD reprimands, "Now Guy, you know those things are bad for you."

Guy responds, "You mean bad for me like attacking Consultants, being hulled by your shuttle, being chased by the Guild?"

PhD just rolls her eyes, shrugs and settles into a couch thinking, *He has a point. Oh, how nice, the couch has a joystick.*

The *Thrill of Agony* rumbles to life and blasts toward the Fly on a vector designed to arc into the radiation interference zone of the Sun. EVAC U8 is good at what he does.

All is going as planned and they're just moments from the reaching the Fly. The Fly is opening and all vectors are vectoring. A Consultant destroyer appears aft.

Over the comport comes their demand, "This is

the Pan-Man-Poo destroyer *Tax Inversion*. Come to a full stop. We need to review your flight records and purpose for this rapid exit of the system."

Needless to say, the Guys aren't in the mood to answer or stop. The destroyer begins to fire on the *Thrill of Agony*.

Guy doesn't hesitate and gives a command with the calm reassurance of someone quite used to running from people and things.

"EVAC ol' buddy."

"Yes, Guy?"

"I don't think we emptied the sanitanks from cleaning up all the spilled Viscean antimatter lube, do you?"

"As a matter of fact, no. Would you like me to take care of that for you?"

"Yes, please, if you don't mind."

A stream of the most disgusting antimatter lube goo imaginable begins to flood from the aft waste tubes of the *Thrill of Agony*. The effect of which is quite disgusting, but effective, as effects often are.

Antimatter lube, and the Viscean's make the finest, has a number of amazing properties. The ones on display here are the way it's engineered to maintain viscosity, even in the cold vacuum of space, and how it interacts with directed energy shielding.

The Consultant destroyer's forward shields are now coated with a brilliant display of vaporizing sludge. It swims, sparkles and flashes like a psychedelic lightning storm.

The resulting release and absorption of energy temporarily blinds the Consultant's targeting systems. Their weapons are now missing the *Thrill of Agony*.

"EVAC. I think the 'zip it in the fly' maneuver is

in order." comes the other Guy's command.

"Zip it in the fly? What exactly does that mean Guy?" the Doctor's face is tense.

"Oh, we'll just close the fly before we're through. No big deal."

"But if we haven't passed through it yet. We'll be zipped alive!" Piobar is now panicking.

"EVAC U8 has a few tricks up his sleeves... uh... data ports. With exact timing, we will be just past the safety limit zone for passing through and the Fly will close. Again, timing is everything. For this to pay off, the Poo destroyer won't have yet entered the approach safety limit zone."

Guy jumps in, "Not to worry Doctor. It's the destroyer that's going to be totaled. The Hyperspace Flies are virtually indestructible and there's no way they'll have time to avoid it. Too bad no one can hear it, going to make one phall of a crunch!"

The *Thrill of Agony* passes through the Fly only a few stanmeters before it completes its thunderous silent zip.

"There, you see. If MOTIV-8 has anything, he has timing skills," comes Guy's command brag.

PhD looks over at Guy with a look of admiration, and not a tiny bit of lust.

On the other side of the Fly, in the Earth's star system, the Pan-Man-Poo destroyer is regaining full forward sensors and visibility. The Captain of the destroyer is yelling commands at the crew to press the attack.

"Get me those damn sensors online NOW! After them, full impulse. You'll pay if they get away!"

Just as the crew is executing his orders, the sensors and visibility return. The Captain looks up in horror just as the destroyer slams into the closed

Fly. The bow of the ship crumples as the Fly absorbs the impact. The Guys seem to have that crumpling effect on the Consultant's ships lately.

"Guy?"

"Yes, PhD."

"I think it might be wise to park us out of sight for a short while. The Doctor and I have had a rough day. A little rest might be in order before we begin another exciting day with a raiding run."

"Absolutely, a fine suggestion."

Guy says, "Good plan." He immerses his hands in the configuration control pads. "I'll configure the *Thrill* to look like an asteroid just for good measure. Let's relax and refresh. Sauna anyone?"

◊ ◊

Supreme Commander Cameron stares at the holoskin screen in front of him. He's trying to avoid eye contact with The Partner. The Partner stares through Cameron as he waits for news. The display lights up with a status report from the captain of the destroyer. His face is red and contorted with anger.

"Supreme Commander, the raiding ship has disappeared. We've been searching using all scanning technology and nothing resembling it has been detected."

"That's preposterous!" comes the response from both The Partner and the Commander simultaneously.

One of the crew of the destroyer appears on screen next to the Captain and gives him some whispered information. The Captain gives him orders and turns back to the screen.

"Supreme Commander, I've just been informed that a different ship has blasted from behind Venus and is vectoring toward the Fly in an odd, but entertaining, flight path. We are going to intercept and question them."

"Get on with it. We need answers!" The Supreme Commander is trying to at least appear to be in control.

As the two wait for an update, the Commander looks around the office for somewhere to hide. Finding nothing, he just stands and stares at the holoskin as if he's willing it to give him good news.

The Partner laments, "You realize this means we'll have to write down the entire *Portfolio* investment. The insurance companies and stockholders will be up my ass like a malfunctioning PleasMech!

"It took us ten stanyears to design and perfect the *Portfolio* class of ships. Some star systems are getting nervous about how deeply we've embedded ourselves into the workings of their business and government sectors. There are rumors of rebellion forming among some of the converts. They won't be as well organized or attractively dressed as our Consultants, but they still pose a threat that should be considered.

"This isn't the first raid on our ships, as you well know. We've lost thousands of stantons of office supplies. Oh the lost profits... the lost profits..." The Partner trails off.

"I've put all Consultant ships on alert. Though the message will take some time to reach the farthest ships." Cameron is using this command lie because the thought has just crossed his mind.

He continues, "I agree with your assessment, sir. Thankfully, we are days away from completing construction of the second of the Portfolio Class flagships, the *Attaché*. This is a huge setback, but it could be much worse. I'll also see to it that our engineers learn from this disaster. We will be deploying a stronger and more dangerous ship this time. We will make the *Attaché* even more formidable than our current battleships. Your grand plan is not in danger, sir."

"Good. Make sure to get an Obscure-Your-Point deck to me with the details. Oh, and don't forget, all the added armament must be invisible to our customers. We can't have it be obvious we're building warships, now can we," The Partner smiles a happy psychopath smile.

Again the holoskin comes to life with an update from the destroyer Captain. The Commander can see in the background that the bulkheads are crumpled, equipment is shorting out and the crew is racing about trying to repair systems and put out fires. The Captain has mild contusions and his, once perfect, pinstriped uniform is now soiled and torn.

"Supreme Commander, the news is not good. The unknown ship managed to close the Fly just as we reached it. We were caught off guard and have crashed into the closed Fly. Preliminary assessment is that we're not so damaged we can't limp back to base for repairs. I'm afraid we've lost them."

The Partner doesn't even allow the Commander time to respond before blowing up. "WHAT the HELL is going on! Am I surrounded by incompetence at the very heart of the most competent organization in all of humanoid history? We've been defeated in our own front yard!"

Again the Captain provides an update. "We've assessed the damage to the Fly. It appears it won't be functional for some unknown amount of time.

"The ancient builders designed them to be self-repairing. However, the systems work slowly. The raw materials have to be gathered from the Sun and passing asteroids."

"SHIT! Now you tell me we're trapped in our own star system indefinitely!"

The Partner kills the holoskin feed and slumps into his leadership couch. It surrounds him in softness and begins to massage him. None of which is having any success in calming him down.

"Get out of my face! You are a bumbler and this close to being demoted to Gardener. Get everyone involved but tell them CAPTURE not kill. Do you understand me!

"Tell them to check Mucus Prime ASAP. It's our only solid lead at this point.

"I want that dashing young man who attacked the *Portfolio*! I want to personally torture him. Do NOT fail to bring a swift resolution to these issues or you'll be tending artificial landscaping for the rest of your career. NOW OUT!"

The Partner is panting, flailing and generally just not a happy camper.

The Commander turns and heads for the closest exit. Something the Commander realizes, as he stumbles out of the office, is that the Hyperspace Flies are also the only way to communicate above light speed. Meaning the news of this catastrophe, and his command lie about putting the fleet on alert, won't be known for some time yet.

He says a silent prayer to the god of tax deductible derivatives that The Partner doesn't realize this.

◊ ◊

"A sauna sounds divine Guy," PhD sounds more relaxed. "Doctor? Guy? Will you be joining us?"

"I, for one, am exhausted my dear. Go right ahead, but do try and get some sleep. We'll be quite busy soon," comes Piobar's reply. "Guy, could you show me to a cabin?"

"Certainly Doctor. I think a nap would do me a world of good as well. Guy, will you configure two guest cabins for our friends?"

Guy starts off the bridge with Piobar in tow then pauses. "Oh, just this once, can you configure the cabins right-side up? We're all a bit too tired for fun and games right now."

"Oh, just this once, I suppose," comes Guy's light hearted reply.

He thinks, *That couldn't have worked out better. Now I have PhD all to myself in the sauna!*

He immerses his hands in the configuration pads. He completes the configuration and now he and PhD head off the bridge toward the crew cabins as well.

"Let me show you where your cabin and the sauna are. We can meet back at the sauna in, say, ten stanminutes?" Guy is being as suave as he can be under the circumstances. Circumstances being that he's standing so close to PhD and anticipating being in the sauna alone with her.

"Sounds perfect Guy. Lead on." PhD is now smiling that playful smile that often leads to some exploration of the effects of physics.

As they walk off the bridge, she daydreams, *I've never been with twins before. Could have some real advantages.*

Guy shows Piobar to his cabin. "If there's anything you desire, EVAC U8 can provide. Feel free to make yourself at home. I'll have EVAC U8 wake us in eight stanhours and prepare a nice meal."

"Excellent, you're a gracious man. So rare in these modern times. I look forward to it. Good rest Guy," Piobar says, as he steps into his cabin.

"Good rest Doctor."

Guy shows PhD where the sauna is, as if it wasn't obvious. The only hatchway in the corridor with a fogged window and a sign above it saying 'SAUNA'. He then shows her to a cabin. Located next to his. Coincidence?

PhD steps, almost skips, into her cabin. Strips off her Dial-Your-Style activity suit. Admires herself in the full-length mirror. Fluffs her hair in overly dramatic slow-motion with a thick air of confidence. Then presses a spot on her neck and dials in short red hair.

"There, something less sweaty, more casual and exciting," she thinks aloud.

She then takes an instashower (30 stanseconds or less, guaranteed). Dons the shortest towel available that still provides a modicum of modesty. Once again admires the near perfect form she maintains as part of her Sisterhood training.

All in a day's formulation. She thinks, as she glides out the hatchway and down the corridor.

Guy rushes into his cabin. He strips off his activity suit and takes a quick instashower. Then he grabs a towel, wraps it around his waist as provocatively as he's capable of and starts to head to the sauna. Pauses, thinks, forgets and then thinks again, *What am I thinking!*

"EVAC ol' buddy?"

"Yes, oh dull one?"

"Can you setup a nice bottle of Slur wine and some light snacks in the sauna for us?"

"Of course. Red or White?"

"The sauna is blue, silly."

"Oh bother, I'll handle it,"

PhD drifts into the sauna and admires the arrangement. It's decorated in a most calming shade of blue. Octagonal shaped with a wet/dry generator in the center. The temperature and moisture levels are perfect.

"Ahhh... now this is more like it. Quest my ass," she giggles under her breath. Dropping her towel and folding it into a cushion, she reclines on the bench in naked perfection.

The hatchway opens and in steps Guy. The first half of a step anyway. The second half is a total fail caused by the sight of PhD naked in the sauna. He nearly face-plants into the wet/dry generator, recovers with a pirouette worthy of a ballerina and lands, with a thud, on the bench across from PhD.

Removing and folding his towel into a cushion, as if nothing out of the ordinary has happened, he greets her, "Ahh... is this not a lovely way to shed the day's stress?"

He's doing all he can not to stare but one eye is always moving to the fun parts no matter how hard he tries.

"It certainly is," she replies in a soft and sultry voice worthy of the pornies.

A ServMech appears and delivers the Slur wine and snacks. Perfect timing from EVAC U8.

"Please, enjoy a snack," Guy says, pouring her a glass of wine. His eyes now riveted upon her ample and perfect breasts. No amount of self-control effort seems to be capable of removing them.

"I can't help but admire your... uhhh... crystal necklace." Not bad, at least he won't seem as creepy for the riveted stare. "Both Guy and I have ones just like it," holding up his crystal. "See? Is that not a weird coincidence?"

"Yes, I noticed. Mine was given to me by my father. The last time I ever saw him. Soon after, he disappeared without a trace. A mystery the family has never solved." A tone of sadness to her voice. "Now, a new mystery."

"I'll be graked! We were given our crystals by our mother a long time ago. She, too, was never seen again. This is something we need to share with Guy. We have a mystery in common."

He's removed his eyes from her breasts for the first time and has just noticed how green and deep her eyes are. The color almost matching that of the crystals.

"I never take it off. One of the last things my father told me was that it can be given, but never taken. 'Never remove it until the time is right.' he said. When I asked further, he said 'You will know when the time is right.' and then he left."

PhD appears to be tearing up, or sweating, hard to say for sure.

"How bizarre!" comes Guy's response. "That's exactly what our mother told us."

She replies, "Oh, probably just silly superstitious nonsense. I wear it to honor him and always do as he says. Nothing more. As a Disciple of the Sisterhood, I have no interest in childish superstitions."

Guy queries, "How did you end up tagging along with an old fart like Piobar on his quest thingy?"

"It's not much of a story really. My life has been pretty mundane, well, until now. After my father disappeared I was pretty lost. I'd completed three doctorate degrees and still didn't have a purpose.

"I heard about the Convent of the Sisterhood and

decided to apply. I scored so high on the entrance exams they begged me to join. After I was graduated from the Convent, and two more doctorates, I felt like it was time to stop studying and start doing something.

"The Doctor and I have known each other for a while. He consults with the Sisterhood on projects now and then. I asked him if he knew of any openings at the university research facility where he works. He took me in and helped me get a nice position and salary. I just went with the flow. Didn't have a true life-plan.

"The quest is something I was unaware of until today. The Doctor always seems to have a cold. Quite annoying I might add. He's been doing research on upper respiratory ailments for several years now and he's convinced that there's a cure out there. I knew he was becoming both obsessed with finding it and frustrated by the lack of help he was getting. I didn't realize it had reached the point where he was willing to steal a Pan-Man-Poo ship. Pretty extreme for an eccentric old academic.

"He suckered me into going with him before I realized I was agreeing. Now that I look back at it, I don't know why I went along. I'm relieved you two showed up when you did. I'd much rather be here with you.

"Guy, tell me about this pirate thing. How did you end up being pirates? You had everyone fooled with the investment analyst act. Or was it an act?" There's a playfulness in her voice that's the voice control techniques with which women are naturally endowed.

"Our parents weren't interested in a normal family life best we could tell. We never understood exactly what they did for a living. They always seemed to have more than enough credits for whatever was happening. They traveled the galaxy and were gone most of the time. Guy thinks they were intragalactic spies of some kind. He likes to think of them as heroes. I think they were jerks for the way they always left us somewhere for years at a time.

"We were just finishing up our education at one of the hundred schools we attended, well, it seemed like a hundred. Mom showed up for the graduation ceremony just out of the blue. I was shocked. Guy was overjoyed. Believe it or not, we graduated with honors. Something we try to play down.

"Mom comes up to us just as we're heading out to party hardy with a large frat group. She takes us aside and tells us Dad has died of old age and she has to go on some secret mission. She gives us the crystals and the next day she was gone. We never saw her again."

PhD interjects, "Oh, I'm sorry to hear that. I never got to know my mother. She left when I was a young child. Dad never would explain other than to say she was involved in something important and couldn't live with us."

"Sorry to hear that about your mom. Parents are hard to understand. It wasn't a real emotional crisis for us, we always had each other and not much of them. She always disappeared sooner or later. Don't get me wrong. When she was around, she was a good mom. Our dad was her fifth husband, at least I think that's right. Don't know for certain how many husbands she's had.

"After that, we burned through what was left of our school funds bumming around the galaxy. We made some credits competing in Sensie gaming competitions. Guy can crush it on Call of Senseless Violence.

"After a while, we had to find something that gave us some consistent income. Given all the education we had, we tried accounting. After all, we're twins and accounting is double entry."

PhD groans.

"Hey, it's hard to make accounting jokes you know.

"Accounting worked OK for a while. That's when we first met Andakosh and got involved with the Guild. We were working a routine audit. Boring as phall work, let me tell you. Then we noticed some shady book work and it pointed to the current leader of the Guild.

"Andakosh was the Lead Accountant back then. He grabbed the opportunity and helped us follow up and build evidence. Andakosh is ruthless, competitive and was determined to run the whole show one day. That part worked out for him. He busted the current leader of the Guild for that accounting scandal and got himself voted new leader by the Guild.

"We were paid well for the work but decided to bail out. Andakosh is a good man overall, but he's in it for himself. Always keep one eye on people like that, and a door at your back.

"It dawned on us that there were easy credits to be made in scams like the one we'd helped Andakosh uncover. So we tried doing confidence schemes. Investment schemes worked pretty well for a while. That's when we met."

"Yes. You were doing a presentation for the research facility retirement fund committee. We lost a lot of credits on that deal but you were nowhere to be found by the time we found out." PhD smiles with an 'I'm not sure it's funny, but kind of now that I know what happened' smile.

"Yeah, after a while, we figured out that the whole con-game business was going to get us killed, or worse. We lost a lot of credits when some of our marks figured out our con and we had to boost fast. Just wasn't the exciting and frigid thing it seems in the Sensies. We laid low for a while hanging around distraction stations, moving around from one to another. We were running out of credits fast.

"We had to come up with something to do to survive. We contacted our Uncle Cheung who was in the shipping business on Ceres in the Earth system. That side of the family goes back thousands of stanyears in shipping. When shipping used ships that sail on water, if you can believe that.

"One story we heard is that our great, great, great…" he starts counting on his fingers. "Phlurg! How many greats was that? Oh, anyway, granduncle. He was the one who controlled interplanetary shipping in the Earth system in the beginning. He discovered the Earth Hyperspace Fly and had a hand in starting the Pangalactic Management Pool.

"Guy and I think that's just a wild story told by the senile old folks. Never found any good reason to believe it, but might be true."

PhD has a look of total fascination. "Guy, I'm just amazed at all of this. What a fascinating life you two have led. Mine is as boring as a baseball game. But yours, WOW!"

"Oh, it isn't that special." Guy is now blushing and thinking about how well this is working for his plan to have some serious adult fun with PhD. *She's eating this up! I'm in solid!*

"Funny thing, we figured uncle would put us to work cleaning ships or something to earn some credits. When we got there he treated us like important guests. All excited to see us.

"He said something strange. That he had the last of the Escher Class Cruisers and he'd been waiting for us to come for it. So matter-of-fact, like he knew. Really odd.

"The *Thrill* wasn't much to look at back then. He'd hidden it for a long time by configuring it to look like a corroded pile of junk. We were cleaning it up and had just restored the main reactors. First time it had been at full power in forever.

"Cheung came aboard and showed us how to power everything up. That's when he showed us what makes the Escher Class so frigid. The morphing capability. He showed us the liquid control pads and immersed his hands in them. A few stanseconds later, we could feel the ship changing. We went outside to look at it. It was the frigidest looking ship we'd ever seen. That's the form we've used ever since as the normal form. Just to honor him. It's how he thinks the ship should look.

"I left them outside and went in. I started fooling around with the liquid configuration pads and the ship changed form to a beach ball. I'd been daydreaming about a beach vacation all day."

"Oh, now that's too funny," PhD is laughing.

"Guy and uncle didn't think much of it. Guy came stomping in and took his turn. Nailed the look uncle liked on the first try. He's just really good at visualization related things like that.

"Uncle took us through a few drills on reconfiguring the ship interior as well. That's the part I like the best. There's almost no limit to how the interior can be configured. Uncle's favorite preset is for one called Classic Chrome. He had a soft spot for the golden age of ship building. Lots of wood panels, bright colors and all the controls are chrome and mechanical. Well, not actually mechanical, they just look that way. Pretty historically accurate right down to the chrome barefoot gas pedal for thruster control."

"I noticed when we were on the bridge. I have to admit, it's pretty classy looking," PhD comments.

"Morphing is about as frigid as it gets once you get the hang of it. I have fun with Guy all the time by rearranging things when he's not looking."

PhD giggles.

"While we were finishing up getting the *Thrill* shipshape, seems uncle had one more surprise gift for us. He came up to us one day and handed us two ornate handles. That's what we thought they were, just frigid looking handles like you'd see on an antique door or something. I asked him what was up with the handles. Guy was playing with his and managed to activate it. He punched a hole in a crate of sea slugs on the loading dock. Made a phall of a mess and he nearly jumped out of his pants right there. Pretty funny.

"Uncle explained they're plasmascimitars. He called them the ultimate personal weapon. He made a big deal out of giving them to us. Said the technology to build them was lost in something called the Hypocrite Wars over a thousand stanyears back. The same for the Escher Class ships. And none made or seen since.

"The hilts are beautiful by themselves. But the ornate green energy blade with its sweeping curves and shimmering inlay make them a mesmerizing vision. They make an impression to say the least.

"Cheung had them genetically keyed to us. We can use them, either one, but no one else can activate them. They can stop a blaster bolt and cut through anything. Easy to pocket as well. Except for the hilt can give girls the wrong impression in tight pants." Guy chuckles a dirty old man chuckle.

"I can imagine," PhD giggles.

"We didn't think much of it until he made us train to use them. That part was no fun at first. He took us to a weapons training room. Kind of frigid. Like a racquetball court only the walls are embedded with blasters. He had us practice fencing moves with each other until we were pretty good at it.

"Then he turned the wall on, set it to ouch, and we practiced using them to defend against blasters. That hurt a lot for a while, but we got the hang of it.

"He couldn't help but have some more fun with us. He made us practice fighting each other and the walls while jumping on a trampoline. That hurt a lot."

"Fascinating," PhD whispers and leans in closer.

"After all that, we had the *Thrill's* systems up and running. All we needed was an AI and we were ready to go. Our uncle said he was tired of, and annoyed with, the AI program on his ship. That's our ol' buddy EVAC U8."

"Hey, did you just call EVAC U8 by his right name?" PhD takes a jab at Guy.

"Yeah, we just play with his name to annoy him. Something our Uncle Cheung said he did all the time and it just seems like such good fun.

"He loaded it onto the *Thrill* and we were set. As we were about to boost, he came up to us and gave us both a big hug. He hadn't done that since we were kids.

"Last thing he said was, 'Take good care of the old girl and she'll take good care of you'. Never quite got that 'girl' part, EVAC has a male personality.

"We headed out to nowhere in particular when it dawned on us, we still had no career path and were running out of credits.

"We were depressed and bored one evening watching pornies in the ship's media room. The one we were watching was *Pirates of Virginity*. You'd enjoy it. It's full of all kinds of great piratey fun and adventure.

"It hit us like a double shot from a mood elevator... Pirates! We were off and never looked back. It's been one adventure after another. No better way to pass a few hundred stanyears."

"A few hundred stanyears?" PhD asks, startled by what Guy has just said.

EVAC U8 interrupts the conversation, "Guy, Guy instructed me to wake them and prepare a wake feast. It's scheduled for only six stanhours from now. Perhaps you two should get some rest."

Guy is about to summon a command reprimand for the interruption when PhD yawns.

She says, "That's probably a good idea. The wine and sauna have made me realize just how tired I really am. Thank you EVAC U8."

"You're most welcome."

Guy does his best to hide his disappointment and demurs with piratey savoir-faire. His mind racing.

Damn RUIN URD8! No wonder Uncle Cheung was so happy to get rid of him! Be frigid... be frigid...

– Four –

Our group of adventurers are gathered in the mess hall of the *Thrill of Agony*. The ServMechs are whirring about serving up a wonderful wake feast. The mess hall is pure classic. Linoleum flooring in white and green alternating squares. Avocado green enameled metal cabinets and appliances, porcelain sinks set in the counter. The chairs have roll and pleat vinyl cushions and the large main table is all chrome with a brightly colored Formica top surface.

"Did you two enjoy your sauna?" Piobar inquires.

PhD and Guy exchange glances. PhD replies, "Yes, we did. After all we've been through, it was nice to relax. I learned a lot about our friends as well. They've lived interesting lives."

Guy blushes as Guy looks at the two of them and gives them a smug little frown.

As they're finishing up their wake feast, the conversation turns to what lies ahead.

"EVAL U8, have you finished the scans of the system?" asks Guy, mumbling with one last mouthful of food.

"Yes, your childishness.

"Of the two main planets, it appears that Ulgvar Nadir is where the Profits are concentrating their efforts. I detect two transport ships. They appear to have only basic defensive armaments. They are sending shuttles of Consultants and supplies to the surface at regular intervals of two stanhours. I detect no destroyers or other military escort in the area." EVAC U8 always gives good scan.

"Perfect!" say they Guys in unison.

"EVAC U8? Can you please fill me in on the planets of the system, dear?" PhD knows how to make friends.

"Of course. The Ulgvar system has two major inhabited planets, Ulgvar Prime and Ulgvar Nadir.

"Prime is a planet that has developed a civilized society where courtesy and refined behavior are the norm. They have a diverse and thriving industrial sector. One of their specialties is producing high quality electronics components.

"Nadir, on the other hand, is the other hand. Nadir's primary industry is pornies. And not much else. Nadir is the type of planet where even fart jokes aren't funny anymore. Unless you're a Farlaph Beast, whose farts are so repugnant they kill most plant life and cause humanoids to pass out cold. Which the people of Nadir find hilarious."

Piobar looks a combination of sad and angry as he sneezes. "ahaa... chooo!... Is it necessary to take this risk right now? We did not sign up to be pirates. My quest is at risk at every turn it seems."

"Oh Doctor, relax. This piratey stuff is such fun. Way more fun than your quest." PhD has the look of an excited child.

She puts her arm around Piobar's shoulders and pulls him in close.

"It's like being in a sensie. Get into it and let's have some fun with the Profits."

Piobar frowns but relents. "I seem to be outvoted here. Please try to avoid getting us killed before I find my cure." He gives the Guys a stern look.

Guy gets command plany, "EVAC, did the MaintMechs complete the repairs to that Consultant shuttle the good Doctor so rudely interrupted our last raid with?"

"Indeed Guy. The shuttle is spaceworthy and I've reconfigured the cargo bay to accommodate a raiding run."

Piobar's face turns a brighter shade of red, "WHAT! No one said anything about using our shuttle for this raid. What if it's damaged again? Beyond repair!"

"Calm down Doctor. We have a plan and we'll be in and out before they realize what hit them. In fact, they'll open the door for us!" Guy is grinning that command grin he gets when he thinks he has it nailed.

"The plan is both elegant and simple," Guy continues, "We'll use a wide arc to avoid being noticed and bring the *Thrill* into a diametric orbit. The planet will blind them to our presence.

"Then we take the Consultant shuttle and arrive at a time when they're expecting a ship to return for another load of supplies. We slide up, they open the cargo hatch and their LoadMechs will load our booty for us.

"Genius, don't you think?"

Piobar summons his best sarcastic tone, "Oh, certainly. What can possibly go wrong?" He trundles off to the sanicube to mope.

"Pay him no mind, Guys. He's just wound up about his quest. Let's get into the spirit of things!" PhD is into this.

She presses a few hidden buttons on her waist sash and her sexy morning kimono transforms into a tailored Consultant Issue pinstriped suit.

Looking her up and down, Guy shares a thought, *Dazzling in every way. Even a stupid Profits suit looks hot on her.*

Guy receives the thought Guy just forgot. He sighs.

"What was the sigh about Guy?" asks PhD.

"What? Oh, nothing." He blushes and turns away trying to find something that at least looks important to do.

Guy turns to the duo and, with a command I'm in charge look, he says, "Guy, you'll stay here and be on watch. We can't afford for anything to go wrong right now. The Guild won't be off our tails until we deliver a cargo.

"PhD and I will man the Consultant shuttle. Configure the *Thrill* to look like a generic cargo ship and take us in."

Guy takes care of manipulating the morphing controls. Guy presses a few buttons on his Dial-Your-Style pirate activity suit and it reconfigures to a clown suit.

"Oh, filjab! Why does this always happen!"

He fiddles a bit more and now he's the spitting image of a young Consultant. Pressed, pinstriped and boring in every way.

Guy flops into a command couch. He lights an eer weed cigarette and mumbles, "Sure, Guy, I'll stay here. NO problem. Nothing special going on.

"EVAC ol' buddy?"

"Yes, Guy."

"Are we in position behind Ulgvar Nadir?"

"Yes. Situation appears normal. No sign of anyone on the planet, or the Pan-Man-Poo, caring what we're up to. From the data feeds, I detect that a new season of *Angels of Epsilon* has just been released. More of the multi-breast double jointed females you so enjoy.

Seems no one is paying any attention to much of anything else. I'll pull some popular trailers up on your holoskin screens."

"EVAC, you do think of me don't you." Guy is touched by EVAC U8's personal touches.

Guy hits the comport button. "Guy. EVAC tells me that we're all set to have a little pirate fun. You're clear to head out."

"EVAC, give them timing and coordinates to blend in with the other transport shuttles."

"As you wish. As if I hadn't planned for that." EVAC U8 just feels he doesn't get proper respect sometimes.

Guy doesn't even notice the rebuke as he settles in to view half a dozen holoskins covered with trailers and previews of upcoming pornies.

He thinks, *I do love the view from here.*

In the cargo bay, Guy and PhD settle into the command couches of the shuttle and lift off and out the bay. They vector into the standard Consultant shuttle approach that EVAC U8 provided. Like clockwork, the automated systems establish a cargo run. The Pan-Man-Poo operational systems link to the shuttle and dock it to a cargo hold.

The LoadMechs begin loading its cargo hold with crates containing a wide variety of Consultant office supplies; Note-It-Note notes, Discretion Shield generators, Holoboards, FlyCom holoskin conference systems, GooAppSoft business software suite cloud servers, cases of hand sanitizer, cases of custom advertising goods (pens, stress balls, caps). Consultants may be boringly over efficient, but they know that free stuff keeps the suckers coming back.

Just as the LoadMechs are finishing up, Guy spies several cases of Caveat Caviar on the far side of the cargo hold.

He steps up to one of the mechs and gives the command, "Mech. These cases are part of our shipment. Load them immediately."

The LoadMech pauses as lights blink and an occasional odd beeping sounds pursue.

After a moment, the mech responds, "Sir, the manifest shows these commodities are for the ship's VIP guests. They do not appear to be part of any known planet bound shipment."

"I don't think you heard me. I am a Consultant and you are to do my bidding," comes Guy's command bravado.

"One moment sir. I have requested confirmation from the Load Master. He is on his way to the hold now. Please stand by," comes the LoadMechs robotic reply. As if a robot has another type of reply?

Guy turns to PhD, "Phlurg, that didn't work out the way I expected. Too bad, I enjoy their caviar. I suppose we'd better bail out of here before the Load Bastard shows up."

"I agree, let's get while the getting is good!" PhD is smiling a childish 'I stole the cookies' smile.

Guy takes a moment to enjoy PhD's face. Even more beautiful when she's enjoying life.

They hustle back to the control center and slide into command couches. Guy prepares to pull away from the Consultant Transport. He manipulates a few pads on the console to release the docking clamps. He gets an error message 'Clamps Locked by Automated Controls. Unable to Release.'

"All right then, Plan B." Guy swivels his command couch around to the weapons controls.

"PhD my beautiful partner in crime?"

"Yes, Guy?"

"Contact Guy and tell him we need a scoop and run maneuver."

"Certainly Guy." PhD sends the message.

Guy is trying to decide which weapon would do the least damage and yet cause the cargo locks to release. He gives up, the shuttle's controls are just too organized for him to handle.

With a burst of PhD-enhanced 'showing off my swashbuckler side', he draws his plasmascimitar and charges the LoadMech. Before the mech can process in incongruence of it all, Guy slices it in half. It falls to the deck sputtering and sparking.

Guy spins around, assess the cargo latch controls. They assess him. A brief tug-of-war ensues as Guy presses buttons and the buttons un-press themselves in defiance.

The Load Master enters the bay. "What's going on here! Who are you and what have you done to my mech?" He activates his subcutaneous comport. "Guards, to the cargo bay, red alert!"

Klaxons begin to sound and the huge outer hatch of the transport begins to close off the shuttle. Without a moment to spare, Guy slashes through the cargo latch controls with his plasmascimitar and dives back onto the shuttle as the hatch jams half shut.

Not realizing that the Consultant ships are safety redundant, he doesn't know that slashing the control only locks it out, not unlocks it. He powers up the shuttles engines, closes the shuttle's hatch and hits full reverse on the thruster controls. With a screaming sound of twisting metal, the shuttle pulls back taking along with it most of the support structure around the cargo hatch. The cargo bay is now depressurizing. As they watch this latest bit of bad luck unfold, the Load Master floats out into space, arms waving.

On the *Thrill of Agony*, Guy receives PhD's message. He pauses the pornie he's watching and assesses the situation. He decides to have some fun with the Consultants. Slipping his hands into the configuration pads, he looks out the forward viewport at the Consultant transport and concentrates. A few stanseconds later, the *Thrill of Agony* is now identical in appearance.

"UNDU L8, give me a scoop and run, now!" Guy commands.

EVAC U8 springs into action. Actually, there are no springs involved. He opens the forward cargo bay hatch, sets the plasmic portal shields to full and maximizes the *Thrill of Agony's* impulse drive. The *Thrill of Agony* swallows the still reversing shuttle and heads for the Fly.

In the cargo bay, the shuttle slides across the deck with a scream of metal-on-metal and a shower of sparks. The force dampeners do their job and grab the shuttle just before it hits the back wall of the bay. The engines are still blasting in full reverse. Pieces of the Consultant transport ship dangling from the docking clamps.

On the shuttle, Guy spins a command brag, "There, my dear, is a perfectly executed piratey move. Nothing really."

"Guy"

"Yes?"

"You might want to kill the engines now," PhD is

trying hard not to make him look stupid.

"Oh... Yes, of course. I was just doing that," his command lies are top notch.

He opens the cargo hatch and extends the ramp. They exit the shuttle with a piratey spring in their step. EVAC U8 has dispatched the LoadMechs. They enter the cargo hold and get to work unloading the booty. Guy looks around at his work with smug satisfaction. Hands on his hips.

Guy then belts out another great command command, "SIMU L8! What do you say we cash in before another cargo gets lost? Set the Fly for the Elttaes system. Then set a course for the Guild headquarters cargo facility. Best speed."

Guy is sitting in his couch watching all this transpire on the holoskin screen view of the cargo bay. He utters a slight giggle and then takes off for the cargo bay to join in the fun.

Piobar bursts from the sanicube. "What's going on! I heard a crash!"

A cloud of invisible toxic gas drifts out of the sanicube onto the bridge. "Doctor! What the phall is inside you?"

"I must see to my ship!"

Piobar and Guy come jogging into the corridor outside the cargo bay. They collide as they both try to enter the hatchway at the same time. Piobar growls and charges ahead. The Doctor is not happy.

"What've you done to my ship!" he demands. His voice duck-like from the mucus build up in his sinuses.

"Now relax Doctor, no harm done and a bay full of great booty. I'm officially a Pirate!" PhD proclaims with a glee that's both childish and sexy.

She then does a provocative little happy dance.

She's spinning around and swishing the sacred E=mc^2 sign of the Sisterhood over her head. She's one happy lady. Both Guys are paralyzed as they enjoy the moment.

Guy command proclaims, "Guess there are no profits for the Profits on this day!"

Everyone just looks at him, no one laughs. Guy heads off, sulking, to his quarters.

"Let me know when we reach Elttaes," he mumbles.

◊ ◊

The *Thrill of Agony* is making its final approach to the Nozama Trading Guild headquarters on Elttaes. Doctor Piobar is pacing about the bridge assailing Guy.

"You MUST stop taking liberties with my shuttle. It has taken me years to plan and execute my quest. All humanoids in the galaxy deserve the chance to be rid of this vermin that invades our sinuses so brutally and without warning. I implore you to assist in convincing Guy to help, not hurt, my quest."

PhD puts a hand on the Doctor's shoulder. "The shuttle is fine and your quest is still fine. We'll be on our way to Mucus Prime in no time." Those voice control techniques of hers are powerful.

Guy is returning the *Thrill of Agony* to its normal form, his hands immersed in the configuration pads.

He chimes in, "She's right Doctor. We're now in a position to get the Guild off our tails. I think I can convince Guy to make a run to the Mucus system once we finish up here. Since we don't have a way, it's not out of our way."

EVAC U8 decides it's time to wake Guy from his nap. He knows this is going to be a stressful day and

Guy should be sharp. He sounds a gentle chime in Guy's quarters. Having no immediate effect, EVAC U8 tries a loud klaxon. That did the trick.

Guy wakes up with a start and is staring at the ceiling of his quarters. Guy has put a giant smiley face made from antigravity Note-It-Note notes on the ceiling. Guy nearly jumps out of his activity suit before he realizes what he's seeing.

"GRAK! That Guy just can't help making me crazy!"

er

He hears a disembodied voice that seems like it's coming from all corners of his quarters.

"EVAC? Are you talking to me?"

"No, sir. I was busy avoiding ships piloted by drunken crews returning from planet leave."

"Uh... OK... then why did I hear 'er' right after I said 'crazy' just now? Who said 'er'?"

"I detect no other being present in your quarters or any other anomalous readings. Perhaps you were awakened from a dream? We're fifteen stan-minutes from landing at the Guild cargo facility."

"OK, I'm up and at it. See you on the bridge,"

Then Guy shakes his head and thinks, *What am I saying, he's not on the bridge, he's everywhere.*

Guy takes a long instashower and heads to the bridge. He strides to his command couch and flips on the comport. *"Thrill of Agony* requesting permission to land."

He gets an angry reply, "You have balls as big as a farlaph beast coming back here!"

"Calm down, calm down. We have a cargo bay full of booty from a raid on a Profits supply transport. More than enough to pay off our debt and profit to spare. Get it, profit from the Profits?"

"No, I don't get it. I'll inform Andakosh of your arrival. If you don't want your head to be his appetizer at dinner, you better be telling the truth!"

Guy shudders at that thought and kills the comport. He also frowns, no one seems to get his profit jokes. He swivels his couch around to face the rest of the group. He pushes too hard and the couch goes not quite in a full circle ending up facing a wall of waveform monitors. He's pretty sure they're laughing at him.

He swivels again. "OK, why don't you three go to the mood elevation station just down the corridor from the landing bays. I don't want to show up with a crowd to an awkward meeting. Even if he's in a good mood, I want to get out of here before he finds a reason to change his mind. So be ready to boost out of here as soon as I'm finished."

"Will do Guy," comes Guy's happy response. One thing that always makes Guy happy is the chance to hang out at a mood elevation station.

As they head down the ramp from the *Thrill of Agony,* the LoadMechs are unloading the cargo. The Guild cargo facility is massive. Mechs of all manner are unloading and loading ships from all the corners of the galaxy. Actually, the galaxy doesn't have corners.

The Nozama Trading Guild is, at least in Andakosh's humble opinion, the most successful of the galactic trading guilds. The Guild's profits run in the multi-trillion credits in a bad year. He runs a tight organization. Believing that giving at least semi-honest deals and leaning on accounts for prompt payment is a better approach than the old cheat 'em and beat 'em.

His buyers get fantastic customer service and

great delivery. His suppliers, like our Guys, always face hard negotiations over costs, but are as loyal as you'll find.

His organization is so tight that rumor has it even the Pan-Man-Poo admire him. Andakosh takes great pleasure in trading in goods acquired from the Pan-Man-Poo any chance he gets. All the while, supplying them with goods that may have been stolen from them. He enjoys poking them in the ribs. He's that good and that fearless.

Andakosh is not an attractive semi-humanoid. Though no one dare ask, he appears to be some odd mix of reptilian and humanoid. Some speculate he's the result of some long ago genetic experiment gone wrong. Bulging eyes that swivel 180 degrees, a pug nose and multiple chins on an otherwise somewhat humanoid face is disturbing enough. His light green skin color, bulging muscular build and six digits on each hand just make him all the more creepy looking. His appearance is intimidating and he uses that to his advantage.

Andakosh is a pure business man and he's easy to get along with when you stay on his sunny side. Cheat him and he'll have you roasted on a spit and served at a banquet.

The Guys get along better than most with Andakosh. He has a soft spot for them since they were abandoned by their parents and they're pirates. Piracy is a profession Andakosh respects. Not in the least due to the fact that pirates can't do business without a middleman. As we all know, it's the middleman who makes the real profit.

Guy marches into the main hall of the Guild. He's using his best pirate bravado to establish a negotiating stance. Trying his best not to show that he's at least a bit worried how Andakosh will react.

The main hall is decorated in all manner of precious metal and stones, a showplace in a galaxy full of showplaces. The floor gleams like a mirror thanks to the PermaShine surface. At the far end, and it's far away, is an enormous desk behind which Andakosh holds court. Over his desk float holoskin screens showing current galactic bid/ask data for millions of products.

Guy strides into a small crowd of traders of every imaginable race, Andakosh notices his approach. "It's about filjabing time you showed up! If you hadn't brought me a cargo, you'd be dinner!"

"Now, take it easy old friend. I'd never cheat the man who makes my living possible. Seriously, I'm hurt that you even thought that for a moment. Oh, and that you tried to blast my ship out of the galaxy." Guy is using his persuasive voice techniques again.

"Enough with the fast talk Guy. You know you only get so much rope before I hang you with it. Don't waste the personal credit you have with me on missed shipments. I had to salvage half that diamond cargo that was floating around the Fly and then pay through the nose to the owners of the Distraction Station for the rest.

"What've you brought me today?"

"We paid a visit to a Profits cargo ship and have enough office supplies to handle your needs for a long time." Guy is selling it now. "You can take what you need for internal use and still make a tidy profit on the rest. It's quite a haul!"

"Guy, you've always had balls the size of a farlaph beast. Raiding a Consultant ship? You make me proud!"

One of Andakosh's chief assistants leans in and whispers to him, "Remember the Trident of Elpis stories that old trader was telling at dinner a few night ago? That Guy has one of the Trident Crystals around his neck."

Andakosh leans back in his couch and strokes one of his several chins. He thinks, *So he does. I can't believe that a crystal has just walked into my office. Not much to look at for as powerful as that trader said it is. Too bad Guy has to be the one walking it in. I kind of like those two.*

He then summons the assistant back and whispers, "I want you to assign a henchman to follow Guy when he leaves. When the opportunity arrives, take that crystal and bring it to me. Try to avoid doing any serious harm to Guy."

"Sorry for the interruption Guy. Where were we... oh, yes, your cargo. I think we can work something out that helps us both. Be aware, the market for office supplies has gone soft of late. Those grak Profits are expanding into all the systems and they manipulate the market in their favor.

"They even tried to outsource our management. I'll have no part of that. They're nothing but thieves in pinstriped suits, not a religion as they want the dullards to believe. Profits my fat butt, they have evil intentions.

"Speaking of the Poo. We've lost contact with the Earth system and ability to jump there. Seems the Fly there is down. You get around a lot. Heard anything about that?"

"Uh... no, can't say that I have. You know Earth, breaking things is what they do best," comes his best command lie.

"True enough." Andakosh laughs. "Will you be

staying for dinner Guy? No, you're not on the menu."

"No, I'm afraid we have a paying passenger who's upset we delayed his quest to make this stop. We'll be taking off as soon as we settle up."

"Oh, sorry to hear. We need to make time to catch up soon. I want to hear about your adventures and this quest sounds interesting."

"Sounds great. We plan on making another raid soon so we should be back to do more business in a stanweek at most."

"Very well then, but plan a longer visit next time. Let me pull up your cargo inventory." He manipulates a system on his desk.

"Looks like you did well. Even after I deduct the overrun on the diamonds and the cost of the damage you did, you still managed almost a million credits net. Here, let me send a clearance voucher over to accounting and you'll be all set. Safe journeys and profitable piracy!"

"Thanks Andakosh. You run a tight organization and it's always a pleasure doing business with you."

Guy heads out of the office hall. He stops at accounting and settles up with the clerk. Then off he goes to the mood elevation station. One of Andakosh's henchmen following him as he walks down the corridors.

The henchman sees an opportunity and makes his approach. He's just about to make a grab at the crystal when several Rent-a-Nymphs come running up and surround Guy.

"Guy! You old dog you. Where have you been? We miss you. We heard you're in trouble with the Guild. Guess, since you still have a head, you must have wormed your way out of it," all talking at once.

The sudden cacophony of nubile hotties has Guy's head spinning. Not because he's confused, his head is spinning as he scans all the beautiful body parts being pressed ever closer. Hard for a Guy to be happier than in a moment like this.

"Ladies! How wonderful to see you. Sadly, I'm in a rush right now. I have to get the rest of my crew and head out on another run or Andakosh will soon have my head on his plate." He's sorry about a fake excuse for once. "We'll play together again real soon, promise."

A collective sigh runs through the group of lovelies.

He heads into the mood elevation station, henchman still in tow. Spots his companions and heads over to get them.

"Guy! I take it all went well with the Guild?" asks Piobar.

"Are we in the clear?" Guy is always nervous when he creates a problem.

"No worries. I handled things. We even managed to bank a million credits to keep." Guy is full on command bragging, his chest puffed out and a smartass smirk on his face.

A hairy arm reaches between the Doctor and Guy, grabbing his crystal. Guy spins around startled. Before either Guy can even grab the hilt of their plasmascimitar, something no one saw coming happens.

The henchman hasn't even managed to pull the crystal free from Guy's neck before his face contorts in excruciating pain and a green glow spreads up his arm. In a matter of a split stansecond, the henchman is vaporized. Not even a pile of dust to mark his passing.

"OK, did not see that coming! We're not waiting to find out who or why. We need to get out of here. Everyone, to the *Thrill!*" His tone both frightened and dramatic. Guy can't help but play up the pirate savior faire, even when he's scared.

They head out fast. Not even noticing the intense scrutiny the little drama drew from a band of Helrisien mercenaries across the bar.

A rough and scary looking variation on humanoid, the Helrisien's are famous for having more weapons than they have hands, and they have several hands. They're genetically engineered for specific tasks.

Thugs, for example, have four muscular arms facing forward and no external genitalia. Their skulls are hard as rock. Snipers have one arm longer than the other and a single, powerful, eye. Their leaders have two arms articulated forward and two backward plus one additional eye in the back of their head. It's almost impossible to differentiate between the male and female of the species. The most obvious sign being that the females are hairier, meaner and nastier to deal with.

All Helrisiens wear little in the way of traditional clothing. Weapons belts and utilitarian items are all they have on. They're covered in tattoos that tell the tales of their kills and adventures. If they live long enough to reach old age, a rare thing, the tattoos cover their entire bodies.

Before the Pan-Man-Poo enlisted them to do their dirty work, dirty work is all the Helrisien's could get. A wretched, ugly and desperate bag of meat civilization. They fight with everyone for any reason and are hated across the galaxy.

What the Pan-Man-Poo gave them is a way to

make a living doing what they do best, kill and maim. Plus, avoid taxes on their income. As a result, without anyone in the galaxy being the wiser, the Helrisien's became the Pan-Man-Poo dark army.

When they're not killing and being killed, they're often seen enjoying NASHIP races and consuming huge amounts of drugs and intoxicating beverages. A fun bunch.

Back in the Guild main hall, Andakosh is informed of what just happened.

"Your Greatness."

"Don't call me that!"

"OK... Boss, we had an issue acquiring the crystal."

"Really? Like Guy is that tough?"

"We followed Guy to the MES and he joined Guy, a beautiful mystery woman and some old man with a runny nose. Luxen circled behind them and made a grab for Guy's crystal."

"Yes, that makes sense. Where's the problem? A brute like Luxen could've taken his head with the crystal." Andakosh is becoming annoyed.

"That's when things went wrong and more than a little weird. The moment Luxen grabbed the crystal he began to glow green. In a split stansecond he was vaporized. A wisp of green vapor was all that remained faster than I could even blink my eyes. Frightening!"

"Hmmm, it appears the legends may be true. I fear our friend Guy won't be with us long once others discover this. I'll have to consider my options. This may be something the Guild wants no part of." Andakosh begins to become lost in thought.

"Oh, and send some office supplies and personal hygiene products to Luxen's family." Andakosh is a benevolent criminal… trader… oh, what's the difference.

Back aboard the *Thrill of Agony*, Guy is wasting no time. "CIRCU L8! Get us out of here now! Set a course for Mucus Prime. Couch-up everyone."

The ship lifts off and turns its back on the Guild cargo facility. One of the Helrisiens is leaning against a crate of Caveat Caviar and notifying his Captain of which ship the group left in.

A stanminute after the *Thrill of Agony* boosts from Elttaes, a Helrisien light cruiser boosts as well.

– 5 –

Guy now takes his first calm breath and begins to wrap his head around all this. "OK, so we three have identical crystals. That's an odd coincidence to say the least. On top of which, they're dangerous. Anyone have any ideas?"

Guy and PhD exchange glances. PhD begins, "Guy and I noticed we both had them when we were relaxing in the sauna. All I know is that my father gave me mine and disappeared never to be seen again. I wear it to remember him."

Guy joins in, "Guy, is that not making weird into weirder? That's pretty much how we came to have our crystals. Mom shows up for no reason, puts them around our necks and she's gone for good."

PhD interrupts, "Oh, and when my dad gave me mine he also put it around my neck. Then he said it can be given, but never taken."

"OK, this is making my brain hurt. That's what our mom said too." The other Guy shakes his head.

Piobar chimes in, "At least we have data to work with: A) There is some connection between the three of you and the crystals that you're unaware of. B) The 'never taken' comment lends itself to the recent discovery that the crystals have incredible defensive power. They recognize the true owner and repel any attempt to take them. C) Your parents are quite irresponsible and just disappear."

In unison, "Hey, lay off our parents Doctor!"

"I'm sorry if I offended. Just trying to analyze the situation. I'm sure you were abandoned for a good reason."

A collective 'ugh' from the trio ends the conversation for the moment. Guy's face lights up. He either has bad indigestion, or just had a brilliant thought.

"COPU L8. Change of plans. Take us to Persei before we head to Mucus Prime."

"Yes, Guy."

"Wait! What!" The Doctor isn't happy with yet another delay.

"Doctor, your analysis of the crystal situation didn't help a bit. However, it did make me realize that if someone is after our crystals we might be followed. We don't want to lead them to you precious cure now do we? We'll take a precaution and end that before it begins, if necessary. A short delay for a long payoff." Guy saw even more whining coming and headed it off.

The *Thrill of Agony* makes the jump to Persei. EVAC U8 cautions, "Remember, Guys, we have to be careful here. The radiation, gravity anomalies and magnetic fields are intense. The rapid rotation of the stars makes navigation tricky."

PhD is gazing at the star system through the forward view ports as they come through. "WOW! That's beautiful. Two stars locked in battle."

EVAC U8 wastes no time showing off. "This is a binary star system. The smaller Phi and larger Persei stars are exchanging gasses. You could say that the giant flattened star is eating the smaller one. Though, in a few billion stanyears, the exchange will switch directions."

"It's quite spectacular to watch. I've never seen a star that's almost flattened out."

"The 'eating' star has an incredible rotational speed and creates immense gravity disturbances causing it to lose the normal spherical shape."

Guy interjects, "We use this spot on occasion to take care of anyone trying to chase us. There's nothing in the stars' system worth having so the only other ships that come here are an occasional tourist cruise or university science cruise." Guy moves to stand close to PhD at the view port.

Guy, on the other hand, is taking care of business. "CUMU L8. Drop a lurking torpedo just off the plane of the Fly. We'll use the standard plan. Take the *Thrill* in as close as you can to the stars and turn us to face the Fly. Set the hull for background matching stealth mode."

PhD looks concerned. "What are we doing?"

"The lurking torpedo is a combination of a mine and a missile. It uses almost no power when lurking so it's indistinguishable from the background crud in space. If we activate it, it only takes a flash of a signal so we don't give away our position. It takes off and vaporizes the closest ship to its location.

"The beauty of this weapon is that it can vaporize the target if it isn't protected by shields. No cloud of debris travelling at incredible speed. Even if their shields are up and at full power, the explosion will disable them enough for us to deal with the situation.

"All I have to do is push this button." Guy points to a blue button on his command couch.

EVAC U8 interrupts, "Uh... Guy... It's the other blue button."

"Oh, right, I knew that. Anyway, we'll hide in the

crazy radiation fields of the stars and be undetectable. We'll use the forward view ports to determine if anyone is coming after us. If they are, they won't last five stanseconds after they come through the Fly."

"Is this really necessary Guy?"

"You having trouble remembering what just happened in the MES?"

"Oh, well, I guess anyone willing to just steal your crystal probably wouldn't hesitate to hurt you to get it. I have to admit, I've lived in a bit of a bubble. I've never seen anyone vaporized, something I thought only happened in Sensies.

"I suppose pirate work has to have a nasty side. All the years of equations scrawled on holoboards has left me out of touch with the actual physical manifestation of reality. It really is a wild and dangerous galaxy, isn't it? I'm being naïve I suppose." She has a look of concerned surrender.

They didn't have to wait long. The Fly activates and a ship comes through. Guy's hand moves toward the, correct, blue button.

EVAC U8 yells, "Tourist Cruiser!"

"Oh Phall! That was close. Grak tourists would come by right now."

Just as everyone begins to calm back down, the Fly activates again. A Helrisien light cruiser comes through the Fly. Since the tourist cruiser is the only ship they can see, they haven't activated their weapons or shields yet.

This time, Guy doesn't hesitate. He hits the button. The Helrisien ship is vaporized only a few thousand stanmeters from the tourist cruiser. The tourist cruiser is shaken but not damaged.

PhD is breathless. "OK, that was both scary and

exciting at the same time. I'm just amazed at how small my universe has been until now."

"You haven't seen anything yet. Stick with us and we'll show you amazing things." Guy is command bragging now.

"And some of them won't try to kill us," Guy chuckles.

"OK, TRUNC-8, time to get back to work. Piobar is looking impatient with the sightseeing."

The Doctor has been staring out the viewport frozen with fear until he hears his name. "Yes, please. I'm trying to be patient but you're trying my patience."

"On to Mustache Prime then!" Guy is now just trying to incite the good Doctor.

The *Thrill of Agony* heads for the Fly. As they pass by the tourist cruiser they can see the tourists in the large expanse of view ports. They're waving their arms and clapping.

"Look at those rubes. They probably think that was part of the cruise package entertainment," Guy grins.

◊ ◊

The *Thrill of Agony* makes its approach to Mucus Prime while Piobar briefs the team on his plans for the visit. "Let me fill you in on the Mucusans. We'll need to be on our best behavior if I'm to get the data they have on a cure. Where do I begin?"

"I like the middle myself," says Guy. "I always falls asleep during long stories."

"Yes... uh... whatever. I have only been able to piece together a thin sketch of what to expect. Little information is available on either the planet or the Mucusan people. They're xenophobic and untrusting of outsiders. This is due, in no small part, to the fact that the entire civilization has had a cold throughout their history. We're talking the longest lasting and most wide spread cold ever encountered in the entire galaxy. Which makes them a prime source for data. And why no one really likes to visit them. ahaa... chooo!... so sorry... sniffle...

"Their societal structure is not what you're used to and we have to be careful. The Mucusans are a matriarchal society. Which means you should demur to the female when in doubt regarding a decision. Guys, be aware that the males will make no secret of their admiration of PhD."

"Doctor, I can handle myself, thank you." PhD is flattered.

"I'll be more than happy to protect her honor!" Guy is turning all piratey again.

"No, that's just my point. PhD will be expected to take care of herself. We, as males, should defer to her in public. Here the men are subservient and considered sexual objects. Which also means that the females may try and pull you Guys into some uncomfortable personal encounters.

"It's important that PhD treat us as owned males to prevent any diplomatic issues. In fact, you should act as though the *Thrill of Agony* is her ship not yours. I want nothing in the way of their being open with their data and progress on the cold."

"It won't be easy, but I think we can handle it Doctor." Guy seems upset. You can tell because he's stopped using his command voice.

"Sounds quite nice for me." PhD is smiling that charming little girl smile again.

"Speaking of the ship. Can you do some of that morphing magic of yours? Configure her to appear as a benign research vessel? No weapons should be visible. Something in a drab gray color, lots of antennas and view ports would be about right."

"Can do Doctor." Guy goes to work at the configuration pads.

EVAC U8 notifies the crew, "There appears to be only one spaceport on the entire planet. I'll take us in."

The others watch the landing through the forward view ports. The planet is about as drab as a living thing can be. Everything, even the trees, seem to be more gray than any other color. A light drizzle is falling from a layer of clouds that flow uninterrupted into the distance.

"EVAC U8, can you put me in contact with the arrival authorities please?" Piobar prepares to present their arrival.

"Communication established with a Professor Posnazal."

"Thank you."

"Professor, this is Doctor Piobar of the Earth science vessel *Thrill of Discovery*. We're on a mission of great importance to the humanoid populations of the galaxy.

"Request permission to meet with your experts regarding your research into the abomination that is referred to as The Common Cold," sounding both official and boring.

Guy whispers in his ear, "Nice idea, *Thrill of Discovery*."

Professor Posnazal replies, "Well, this is a bit of a surprise. We weren't expecting guest. Are you certain you've come to the right planet?"

Piobar mutes the comport. "You see. As I said, they're not welcoming of strangers. We'll have to put her at ease."

PhD interrupts, "Doctor, let me take over. I think we need to establish a female lead here."

"Good idea, please."

Unmuting the comport, PhD takes over. "Professor Posnazal, this is Doctor Prudence Hortense Dincheimer, leader of our expedition. I apologize for being late for our first contact."

"Doctor Dincheimer, I see. No apology necessary."

"Oh, please. Everyone calls me PhD. Much easier to say."

"As you wish."

"I feel certain that a sharing of data on this sinus destroying scourge will be of mutual benefit. We've visited researchers on many planets. We've encountered so many dead ends in our research. You may have the key data we're missing to finally make progress. We won't disrupt your quiet existence any longer than necessary."

"If you insist. I'll arrange a meeting. My assistant, Driznia, will meet you at your ship with protective masks for your visit. She'll give you a brief tour and show you to our conference facility." She then cuts off the comport link."

"OK, not very talkative are they?" PhD is put off by being cut off.

They deship and are met at the end of the ramp by Driznia. She's tall and slender with striking facial features but her complexion is as gray as the rest of their surroundings. Mucusans are not into sun bathing, assuming the sun ever shines.

"Welcome to Mucus Prime. I am Driznia. I'll be assisting you for the short time you're here."

She reaches out to the group and hands them each a rather sleek and stylish protective mask.

"Please press this against your face and it will adapt to your facial structure."

PhD is startled by how it morphs to a perfect fit over her eyes, nose and mouth.

"My, this is advanced and comfortable," she says, with a slight muffle to her voice.

Driznia then turns and leads them into the facility. As they pass other Mucusans, they're given polite and interested glances. Females are eyeing the Guys. PhD pulls them into line behind her with a defiant flourish. Making certain to make eye contact with the admiring Mucusan ladies.

A couple of males in lab coats pass them walking the other direction. They turn and admire PhD long enough that they bump into each other. PhD notices this and gives them a coy side glace that projects both approval and get on your way.

The walls in the hallway that leads to the research center have tissue dispensers and disposers placed every few stanmeters.

"That's convenient. They think of everything here don't they Doctor," Guy comments.

"Yes, a civilized society dealing with a chronic condition. I'm certain they have research that will be of value to me."

Driznia leads the group to the large windows overlooking a laboratory. "Here we're working on various advanced decongestants. In order to stay ahead of the rapid adaptations of the cold virus, new compounds have to be formulated constantly."

Piobar interjects, "We've seen the same results on Earth. A constant game of whack-a-mole."

Driznia looks at him. "Whack a what?"

"Oh, just an Earth expression for something that changes as fast as you figure it out."

"How quaint." She leads them to another laboratory. "Here we're working on aerosols to control respiratory congestion centering in the lung area."

The Guys are doing all they can to look interested. A difficult task for them. Piobar is nodding.

PhD comments, "These labs are extraordinary. I see you have unusual and unique apparatus among the more familiar. Do you develop your own technology as well?"

"Yes. We gather data from across the galaxy and try to enhance it. Many of our attempts fail to produce positive results, however."

PhD thinks, *Driznia's lack of detail seems evasive.*

Piobar wanders to a lab area where the windows are tinted out. "Driznia? What's in this area?"

"I'm afraid that's off limits for tours. Specific work is being done that cannot be revealed at this stage. Moving on," she ushers them toward large double doors at the end of the corridor. Our group give each other quizzical glances.

They enter the main conference room. Seated at a large conference table are four female scientists. In the back of the room, two males are tending to drinks and snacks laid out on a side table. The ladies are admiring the Guys.

The Guys share a quick thought, *Do love it when the ladies are checking us out. Too bad they're so dull and gray.*

The eldest of the women greets them, "Welcome to Mucus Prime. I am Professor Posnazal," she extends her elbow in greeting.

PhD steps forward, touches elbows with her. "Thank you for meeting with us. I'm PhD, this is my collaborator Doctor Piobar and these gentlemen are the commanders of my vessel, Guy and Guy."

Piobar touches elbows with Posnazal. The Guys bow and step back toward the snack table. Which is something they're actually interested in. Of course, they start snacking immediately.

Posnazal chastises, "Now gentlemen, please wait until the ladies have selected their nutrients." She motions to the doctors, "PhD, please go first."

The doctors and the Mucusans settle in around the table with their snacks and drinks.

Posnazal inquires, "Tell me doctors, what makes you think we can be of service in your research."

Piobar begins to respond but then takes a cue from PhD's sideways glance and demurs to her.

"Professor, the good Doctor and I have visited many planets in search of a cure. More than once the Mucusans came up in our conversations with other researchers. It seemed logical to come here and determine what progress you've made on eradicating the problem. From what we gathered, there is no group in the galaxy who has focused more research effort on the problem."

Another of the Mucusan scientists responds, "That would seem logical. As you've already discovered, the thing you call the common cold is indeed common among humanoids. We've identified few viable avenues toward an overall cure. Sadly, none have panned out. The best we've been able to do is lessen the severity of the symptoms."

Piobar now joins the conversation, "We've noticed you seem to suffer milder symptoms. I do, however, find it hard to believe that in all your years of research you haven't found any successful way to obliterate the virus."

Posnazal says, "Doctor? Are you insinuating that our work has been inferior in some way?"

"NO! Heavens no. It's just that we've studied data from a thousand worlds and everyone seems to hit a dead end at some point. I just find that so odd in such a technologically and scientifically advanced galaxy.

"For example, I've been working on the design for a treatment using focused scanning neutrino reflective bilateral bombardment of the upper respiratory tract.

"It seems like every time I get close to finalizing a piece of the design puzzle someone comes along and asserts it won't function. They point out some obscure flaw in the design. Systems that should be working inexplicably fail during tests.

"It's almost as if there's a conspiracy of some kind to prevent progress on total eradication. Odd, don't you think?"

At the mention of Piobar's plans, the Mucusans lean in to each other and murmur. Piobar and PhD try to listen in but can't make out what they're saying. Not in the least due to the fact the Mucusans noses are plugged making their language even harder to understand.

After a few tense moments, Posnazal touches her neck just behind her ear. She murmurs something. She's using a subcutaneous comport to communicate with someone not in the room.

Piobar and PhD glance at each other. The Guys rest their hands on the hilts of their plasmascimitars.

Piobar can't stand the suspense any longer and begins to demand answers. Not realizing that someone is entering the room behind them.

"Now please! It's clear that you're doing your best to share nothing with us. A tour with no real details. Mystery labs with blacked out windows. What is going on?"

From behind him comes an old and cold sounding voice. "Good Doctor. Please calm down."

Piobar and PhD spin around to see who's speaking. Without a sound, an elderly Mucusan woman dressed in regal robes has entered the room. She's staring a hole through Piobar.

"Let me introduce myself. I'm Vapo Rubia. I'm the Queen of Mucus Prime. Your assertions have created a great deal of anxiety among my scientists. I think it's time we have a frank discussion."

"Now we're getting somewhere!" Piobar leans forward in his chair.

Vapo Rubia continues, "Perhaps. But not where you may think we're getting. You see, my other role is the leader of the society responsible for preventing the discovery of a cure for the cold."

Confused and curious looks spring out like bad acne on the faces of our group of adventurers.

"We have existed for thousands of stanyears hiding in plain sight on humanoid planets across the known galaxy. We insinuate ourselves into leading research teams related to upper respiratory distress. Doing our best to mislead and distract any effort that shows promise."

Piobar is now confused and babbling, "But... But... I just don't understand. Why would you want to prevent such a wondrous miracle as the elimination of this vermin?"

"Please, calm down Doctor Piobar. And know your place, male!

"It's quite simple. We're protecting an advanced race of nanobeings from genocide."

Her words fall like the final curtain at a grand

stage production. Piobar slumps into his chair trying to wrap his mind around what's just happened.

She continues, "The cold is the result of a natural immune reaction to the interdimensional transportation system used by the Anosmian race. They're advanced beyond our comprehension and travel through the multiverse in small colonies doing scientific research. The mucus produced by their transport is vital to their survival as both a food and a living environment.

"Therefore, Doctors, curing what ails us would be genocide. There's no way to eliminate the effect on us without killing them by the millions. Everything about their lives in our universe is related to the mucus produced in the humanoid hosts.

"Over the many stanmillennia, our race has been secretly dedicated to protecting them from annihilation. A secret we've now shared with you due to your assertions.

"Doctor Piobar, your device would not only kill the Anosmians living in our sinuses. It would have unfortunate consequences for anyone within thousands of stankilometers. If the Anosmians are in the process of interdimensional travel when such a device is activated, it would rip space-time. Before they could react to control the rip, it would warp all nearby mater into unimaginable forms."

Piobar is still trying to succeed. He tries consequences as a tack. "But Your Greatness, are they not attacking us in a hostile manner? Humanoids come down with numerous complications, pneumonia for example, from the effects of the Anosmian infestations."

"Yes, Doctor, you're right. There are unfortunate side effects to the Anosmian way of living and travel. However, these are minor and becoming much more rare thanks to the countervailing symptom reduction techniques they've helped us develop and spread across the galaxy.

"For us, the Anosmians are gods. They can travel through the entirety of all universes. They're peaceful in all ways and curious beyond belief. They also have a fascination with pornies, for some odd reason."

Piobar slowly removes his mask. "I suppose these are just a ruse as well."

The Guys and PhD come to the same realization and remove their masks. Moving slowly as if processing the information and acting on it at the same time is too much effort.

PhD now regains her composure and joins the discussion, "You can communicate with them?"

"Certainly my dear. The Anosmians initiated communication with humanoids almost at the dawn of modern evolution. How do you think we developed fire, tools, society in general? They needed us to be warm and well fed. I assure you, this has been a symbiotic relationship.

"They're very selective about who they communicate with. They're cautious not to do any harm by what they reveal to the races they encounter. They have revealed only the most crucial advancements at the most critical times. Otherwise, they allow beings to advance at their own pace. They know, too well, the consequences of helping a race to advance beyond their grasp.

"Which, if I may interject a bit of humor, is why the humanoids of Earth are so far behind those of other planets in the galaxy." She chuckles cautiously, hoping to break the tension in the room.

Piobar scolds, "You seem to be keeping a lot of secrets. Like the lab with the blacked out windows. What secret is hiding there?"

Vapo Rubia gives him a look that combines contempt and resignation. "If you must know, insulant one, we're testing a technology to allow Anosmians to exist outside our sinuses. Providing them with a safe space in which they can congregate in much larger numbers than a typical humanoid sinus allows."

The Guys have moved to stand on each side of PhD. They're both fascinated by what's transpired and the snacks are all gone. Guy leans over and sneaks a few last tidbits from Piobar's plate.

Vapo Rubia's face goes pale, even paler, and all expression disappears from her face. She appears to be in deep and desperate thought.

Unbeknownst to the group, while Guy was preoccupied with sneaking snacks, his crystal slipped out between the collars of his activity suit. Vapo Rubia is staring at the crystal.

She says, "That crystal you're wearing, it's beautiful." She points at Guy's chest.

Guy speaks up, "We're rather fond of them. Though we just had a strange experience regarding the one Guy wears. Someone tried to steal it. When he grabbed it to yank in from Guy's neck, he was vaporized. Weird and frigid at the same time."

"And ruined our mood," chimes in the other Guy

"You say we and them? How many do you have?

PhD says, "The three of us have them." Pointing at the Guys and herself.

Vapo Rubia's face is now even more incredulous at what's transpiring before her.

"You have no idea what they are?" Vapo Rubia is

fishing for what they know rather than telling what she knows.

PhD chimes in, "No, not really. All we know for certain is that our parents gave them to us. Oh, no, we aren't related. Their mother gave them theirs and my father gave me this one.

"Both our parents told us the same thing though. They said 'The crystals can be given but never taken.' Does that make any sense to you?"

"Ahhh... yes, it does. Though I'm afraid I won't be of much help. The Trident Crystals are shrouded in mystery. There's only so much I can share."

"Trident Crystals?" Guy asks.

"Yes. They're the crystals that empower the Trident of Elpis.

"They're powerful and of huge importance to the future of the galaxy. Once bestowed upon a bearer, that would be you three, they're capable of protecting the bearer from harm. I know that they're a critical part of your destiny."

She thinks for a moment and then adds, "There may be value in your traveling to Angstuvia in the Nervosis System. There's a shop in the city of Paniclateris named A Penchant for Crystals that specializes in exotic crystals. Perhaps you can find out more about your future there.

"One thing you should be aware of is the legend:
> The bozos and the babe will make a show.
> The winds of change will blow.
> When the three are on a tree.
> They will set the galaxy free."

Piobar isn't happy with either the change of subject or the ominous sound of that. "Well! That's just about useless information. And pretty lousy poetry as well!"

Vapo Rubia's eyes betray that she's considering having Piobar punished. "That is enough insolence from you!"

With that, she dismisses the lot of them. "It's time for you to leave Mucus Prime. You've learned all you can learn. If you share any of what we've told you about Anosmians, you will suffer dire consequences. Is that clear?"

She turns, without waiting for an answer, and glides out of the conference center followed by the other Mucusan scientists. Our heroes all look at each other in astonishment and confusion.

Piobar is the first to break the silence, "Well, what a grand day this has been! My quest has fallen flat like a fart joke on Ulgvar Nadir and yours, it appears, has just begun. I'm going back to the *Thrill* and sulk in my shuttle."

Driznia leads them back to the landing pad and bids them farewell. "Do not underestimate our wrath. Your silence is NOT a request. Are we clear?" Without waiting for an answer, she turns and strides away.

"These people love to ask questions and then not wait for an answer?" Guy chortles.

They board the *Thrill of Agony* and Piobar has already come to a conclusion.

"Guys, PhD, there really is no further need for me on your journey. Perhaps in the galaxy as a whole." He sounds depressed and lost. "You have a quest for which I'm entirely unsuited. I must try to reassess my life."

PhD tries to console him, "But Doctor, your life is fine. You have a great many things to contribute to the galaxy beyond a cure for the cold. You're a biochemical genius and you'll find a new quest."

The Guys chime in, "Yeah, what she said!"

"Thank you for your words of encouragement. I'm sure you're right. I think it's best if we part ways for now. I can take the shuttle and return to Earth. You need to be on your way to Angstuvia post-haste."

The Guys are both excited by their new purpose in life and, most important, getting to spend more time with PhD without the Doctor always interfering.

Guy says, "Yes, Doctor, that's a fine idea. Take some time to reflect on your life and ambitions. I'm certain you'll find a new challenge that suits your immense intellect." That command lie is a doozy.

The *Thrill of Agony* boosts from Mucus Prime. Piobar is in the shuttle making ready to depart. Over the shuttle's com system, some depressing classical Earth music is playing.

PhD comes in to say her goodbye. "Doctor? Don't you think some more upbeat music would be better right now?"

"No my dear, sometimes one needs to bask in their failures. Amazing new ideas have come from the edge of despair."

"I'm sure you're right. Are you all set to start your new journey?"

"Yes. Not much to prepare. I'll drift away from the *Thrill* and allow you to transit first."

"All right then. Give me a hug for good luck." She's going to miss the Doctor and it shows on her face.

They exchange polite hugs. Then Piobar makes some less than polite moves with his hands.

PhD pulls away, "Now, now, Doctor. Time to go."

"Excuse me. Just an old man's folly.

PhD smiles and exits the shuttle. She hears one more 'ahaa... chooo!' and she can't help but giggle. Much funnier now that she won't have to hear it every few stanminutes.

Guy's voice comes over the comport. "Whenever you're ready Doctor."

"Thank you, both of you Guys. I appreciate your help in reaching Mucus Prime. Sorry about denting the *Thrill.*"

EVAC U8 has the last words, "Doctor. We're ready to open the bay when you are."

The Doctor presses a pad on the console and the shuttle's entry hatch slides shut. He takes one last look into the bay at the retreating PhD.

He thinks, *Hmmm... going to miss that view*.

"Open the bay EVAC U8, I'm on my way home."

The bay hatch opens and the Pan-Man-Poo shuttle lifts off the deck and drifts out to a safe distance from the *Thrill of Agony*. Piobar is waving in the forward view port, unaware that no one aboard the *Thrill of Agony* is paying any attention.

Aboard the *Thrill of Agony* there's an air of excitement among our heroes. PhD is glowing with the idea of a grand adventure that doesn't involve snot.

"Guy, do you think we've had enough of the drab and dull research ship form?" asks Guy.

"Absolutely right Guy," Guy replies.

He slips his hands into the liquid configuration pads and the *Thrill of Agony* changes back to the awesome normal form.

"Much better, thanks."

Guy gives the command, "TITIL L8. Set the Fly for The Circus and takes us through."

"As you command. Couch-up." Comes a terse reply. EVAC U8 will never grow accustomed to the

Guys' insistence on making a word game out of his name.

"The Circus? I thought we were off to Angstuvia?" PhD looks confused. "Do we have time to go to a circus? Where is this circus anyway?"

Guy responds, "No worries my dear. The Circus is the planet Grimaldia in the far reaches of the galaxy. It's our secret pirate hideout. You know how it goes, pirates have to have a code name for home. Can't go around using the real name of the planet, now can we. Wouldn't stay secret long."

The Fly unzips and the *Thrill of Agony* fires up full impulse power. In a flash, they're through the Fly. Piobar is watching from the shuttle. He's awe struck by the thunderous zip sound it makes as it closes, and he can't hear.

◊ ◊

In Supreme Commander Cameron's office, on Earth, things are more than a little tense. He's destroyed one 'Pan-Man-Poo Gives You Strength' stress ball and is working on the second. The Hyperspace Fly has been offline for several days now and he hasn't been able to fulfill his lie, uh, promise to The Partner.

He thinks, *If I can't get a message out soon I'll be tending plastic roses the rest of my life.*

He's staring at a holoskin so intensely the screen is wincing.

"What's the status today? Please tell me we have at least FlyCom working!"

The officer on the other end of the connection is sweating. "We've been checking stanhourly sir. I'm sure it will be back online soon."

"Stanhourly! I want you to check it stanminutely. In fact, check it NOW!"

"Not up yet sir."

"Again, NOW!"

"Sir? Yes, sir."

There's a brief pause and the officer's gaze becomes focused. He flips some switches and types commands into the system.

His face lights up. "Sir, great news! One system test just came back positive. It appears we have full FlyCom."

"And jump capability?"

"That still shows amber. However, that's an improvement. This morning it was showing red. We should be capable of using the Fly soon."

"Fine. Cameron out."

Cameron has to make some fast arrangements. He knows that all his ships are utilized but the Helrisiens are always ready to jump on a cash deal. He decides it's time to contact Commander Slit, leader of the Helrisien military.

He quickly dials a code and the holoskin image changes to show an ugly Helrisien. Actually, is there another kind? In the background, the bridge of the ship is lit with a dim red glow. The controls look as though the designer was angry at having to design controls at all. The crew at work in the background are all armed to the teeth, muscle-bound and scared.

"Hello Cameron. What work do you have for me today?" He knows Cameron never calls him to check on his health.

"I'm transferring some vid from a recent attack on one of our ships. An internal view showing an old man sneaking onto one of our shuttles. A vid of a pirate demanding surrender of our ship. Some rather fuzzy vid and scans of the pirates' ship.

"I want you to hunt these people down. I'm not too concerned about the old man, we'll get to him. He's only important because he was taken by the pirates and may have information we need. The critical job I have is for you to find these pirates."

"Oh, that shouldn't be too hard. I can have a team vaporize them for you no problem. No extra charge." Slit smiles, well, it might have been a smile. With a face that ugly, it's not easy to tell.

"NO! Do NOT vaporize them. The Partner is boiling mad. He wants them brought back to Earth. He wants to personally torture them to death. Something even you should fear. He's creative in that way."

"Hmmm... so just capture them and deliver them. OK, not as much fun. Standard daily rates apply, unless they damage something. Expenses are as incurred."

"That's fine. Spare no expense to find them. All our heads will be decorations at the Pan-Man-Poo office complex if this doesn't happen FAST!"

"I have some intel that may help you regarding the first place to look. The old man is Doctor Piobar from Earth. He's been petitioning us to help him with research on the common cold. He has a keen interest in going to a planet called Mucus Prime. I suggest you start there and see what you can find."

"I'll send one of my ships to check out Mucus Prime now. Can't say I've ever seen you frightened Cameron. Interesting." He cuts the connection.

"That Slit is annoying. But he never lets me down," Cameron mutters as he kills the holoskin and breathes a huge sigh of relief. He slumps in his chair taking deep breaths to try and slow his heart rate.

His holoskin bursts to life and the zoomed in face of The Partner appears, filling the screen. Cameron jumps with a jerk that almost makes him fall out of his chair.

"Do you have a status on our attackers for me?"

"Yes, sir. I've just been in communication with the Helrisiens I sent to search for them. They haven't located them yet but anticipate they will soon. They're on their way to Mucus Prime now."

"Good. Do not fail me Cameron!"

With that, The Partner's face is gone and Cameron is sitting frozen before the blank holoskin screen. Slowing his heart rate is no longer likely.

He thinks, *Hurry Slit... Hurry...*

– VI –

The *Thrill of Agony* slices out of the Hyperspace-Fly into the Grimaldian system. Guy continues explaining to PhD, "We figured out that pirates need a secret place to hide when things get messy. And the *Thrill* needs a place to rest and be repaired.

"We found this lovely little planet that's perfect. It only has one habitable land mass. A small continent with an enormous extinct volcano surrounded by a global ocean. A friendly, and a little odd, civilization lives on it. They love us to death because no one ever visits them. You'll enjoy it. Think of the Caribbean on Earth only this is an entire planet with no other land but the continent you're on. Warm breezes, warm blue water, not too hot or too cold."

"It does sound nice. But what about getting on with finding out about the crystals?"

"Oh, no worries. We won't stay long. We have to drop off some cargo and do some of financial manipulation. While we do that, EVAC will put the MaintMechs to work making the *Thrill* perfect again. Believe me, it's a worthwhile stop to make when we don't know what we'll encounter next."

"I guess that's logical. I do miss the sea breezes in my hair." She presses that spot on her neck and the flowing blonde hair returns.

Both Guys just freeze for a moment. Making sure

that sight never leaves either of their minds. No need to share this thought.

EVAC U8 announces, "On final approach to The Circus Guys."

PhD is looking out the forward view ports as they come gliding down over the planet. "Oh my word! Those are the bluest waters I think I've ever seen. Your description doesn't do it justice."

They are approaching a landmass that stretches beyond the horizon. Lush green rolling hills are dotted with small cities and industrial complexes. Gentle waves lap the volcanic rock shoreline like puffs of clouds rolling ashore. Spread along the volcano's cliffs and the rolling hills that lead to the sea is the largest city. Sparkling towers try, but fail, to compare to the spires of the volcanic mountain backdrop. There's a seaside resort with yacht club marina that seems to go on forever.

"Yep, pretty filjabing nice," comes Guy's boastful reply.

"Must you always swear Guy!" comes Guy's command admonition.

"Oh, I don't mind. I figured it's a piratey thing," PhD is giggling that sexy giggle again.

They appear to be flying straight at the volcano.

"Uh, Guys, shouldn't we be slowing down and landing someplace smooth?" PhD is concerned.

"Oh, this is the most fun part. EVAC loves this part. Watch." Guy is now in full piratey showoff mode.

"Ready to land Guys?" EVAC U8 is now in the mood to show off.

"Make it so ol' buddy," the Guys reply, in unison.

PhD is at the main forward view port and looking more and more anxious. Only a stankilometer from hitting the volcano, a huge opening appears in the side of the volcano. Inside, landing lights are blinking on in linear strobes on a polished granite floor. Interior lights are coming on revealing a massive cavern.

The *Thrill of Agony* glides onto the landing strip. Spirals of crystalline stalactites hang from the immense ceiling lit by intense internal flood lighting.

"WOW! You two sure know how to pick a place to hang your hats!" PhD can't stop staring. "The way those stalactites glow to light the place. A way cool idea."

The *Thrill of Agony* comes to light in the center of the largest portion of the cavern. Surrounded by banks of work benches, machinery of every description, crates of cargo and a large man cave setup.

Guy activates the comport. "Squeaky, this is Guy."

"Hello Guy! Welcome home," Squeaky replies.

"We're here for a short visit. We did manage to bring you some gifts from our travels. Can you meet us on the front porch in a few minutes?"

"Absolutely, see you soon." He ends the connection.

"EVAC. Have the LoadMechs take our gift for the Grimaldians down to the front porch. Take whatever time you need with the repairs. I want the *Thrill* good as new and sparkling when we leave. Make sure all weapons systems are at peak and all torpedoes are restocked," Guy commands.

"As you command," comes EVAC U8's reply.

Then he verbalizes a command of his own. Showing off? An AI would do that?

"Come to me my little masseuses, let me feel you healing my wounds." EVAC U8 enjoys being home.

"Let's leave EVAC to his little pleasures. Come on, we'll show you around and meet the locals." Guy is in full host-mode.

PhD's impression is stark admiration as she sees the *Thrill of Agony's* normal form from outside for the first time.

"Whoa! The normal form of your ship looked cool on the holoskin but standing here on the ground looking up at her is just, well, awe inspiring. She's just beautiful!"

From inside the ship, she hears EVAC U8 say, "Thank you PhD."

She spins around to take in the massive cavern and is again overwhelmed. "I have to say, this place is just too cool for words Guys. So well furnished and tidy. Are you sure YOU live here?" She's teasing them with her voice control techniques.

"Oh, go on now. We do love it here and we've had the luxury of stealing... um, borrowing... um, acquiring... a lot of nice stuff over the stancents.

"See, look over here. We have our perfected man cave area. Huge holoskins and the Klipsch speaker system can rock the rocks! A deluxe mood elevator with all the options. The finest entertainment couches in the galaxy. No feature or function you can want in a couch is missing." Guy is puffed up so hard he may burst at any moment.

"Down those tunnels are living quarters, a gourmet kitchen and health spa. Down those are machine rooms, parts storage and the freight elevator." he points out the large smooth tunnels drilled into the volcanic rock. They're lit by glowing crystalline structures.

"Wow, when does this place stop getting more impressive. Wait, stancents?" PhD is now sure she heard that. "What do you mean? You made a comment about three hundred stanyears when we were in the sauna."

Guy looks at Guy, Guy nods a knowing agreement. "Since we share the crystal mystery, and you're the only one in the galaxy who knows about The Circus, I suppose there's one other thing you might as well know. Guy and I are three hundred fifteen stanyears old about now."

"Ok, that does NOT compute. You don't look a day over thirty-five! How is that even possible?" PhD looks lost now.

"It is possible. We just don't like to talk about it. It can be a blessing and a curse. The fewer people who know, the better. Guy, you tell it better. Would you?"

"Thanks. You're always monopolizing the story time.

"You see, our mother is Perdurablian. Have you ever heard of that race of humanoid?"

"No. Please, explain."

"Perdurablians are extremely long lived beings. A race that tackled the issue of aging back many stanmillennia ago. They developed an evolutionary fork through advanced genetic engineering. Their lifespans approximate the Lindy Effect. They have no predetermined lifespan. The longer they live, the longer they will live."

"I'm familiar with the Lindy Effect. Amazing to see it playing out biologically!"

"Purebred Perdurablians live, with minor exceptions, until they die. They mature until they reach their mid-thirties and then physical changes just stop. No gray hair, aching bones, heart disease, you get the idea."

"It's soaking in slowly. I'm beginning to realize there's a lot about you two that's amazing.

"Wait a stansec, I remember now. Early in my time with Piobar, he'd just returned from another Conference Against Aging held on the California Islands. He was furious about a pair of twin scientists who presented themselves as biochemists and the leading researchers on aging.

"Piobar was livid when he discovered that their presentation lead a great number of his colleagues into blind alleys. The data they supplied contained false information. He complained they'd set back their research by a hundred stanyears.

"That was you two? That's why he recognized you right away. You were trying to hide what the Perdurablians discovered weren't you?"

"We were trying to lead them astray. For good reasons. For one, we know the reality of long life and it sucks. For another, if the wrong people found out about us they might try to dissect us, or worse. It's best if the galaxy thinks Perdurablians are a myth or long gone.

"We're quickly becoming long gone. Once Perdurablians achieved such long lives, they lost interest in reproducing. Not wild sex, mind you, just the babies part.

"They also discovered that living, essentially, forever doesn't guarantee that you'll have anything to do for all those years.

"They have a high suicide and divorce rate starting about a thousand stanyears in. The lucky have the talents or skills to take on stanmillennia-long enterprises. Some take on extreme sports or adventuring hoping for a quick and thrilling end. Pirate happens to be working for us. Over two hundred fifty stanyears and not a hint of boredom yet." Guy smiles a proud smile.

"No kidding! I haven't had a dull moment since we crashed together," PhD chuckles.

"Our mother is part of a rogue faction who seek out disorder in the galaxy. The rogue faction was ostracized for interbreeding and seeking out wild and illogical adventures. The elder Perdurablians felt it was an insult to all they'd achieved.

"We're only half Perdurablian. The best we can hope for is another seven hundred or so stanyears."

"I'm beginning to think you two will never run out of surprises for me." She smiles.

Guy interrupts, "Enough of that. Let's head down to the front porch and say hello to our friends the Grimaldians. You'll find them enjoyable."

They walk over to a magnalift and descend for what seems to be thousands of stanmeters, because it is. On the trip down, Guy fills her in on the Grimaldians.

"Don't show any surprise when you meet our native friends. Their appearance takes some getting used to but they're wonderful people. Oh, and don't call this place The Circus in front of them. To them it's Grimaldia and they're a proud people."

As the magnalift doors open, PhD can see a group of humanoids standing around the crates the mechs have deposited. And they do take some getting used to.

They're average height humanoids. Their hair is every shade of the rainbow. Some have green, red or blue plus various combinations of all colors. Their feet are large and out of proportion to the rest of their bodies.

Their facial structure is what stands out the

most. It appears that the relaxed state of their faces is a huge smile. The bright red cheeks and large eyes just intensify the effect.

"Ok, Guys. These people look like clowns!" PhD blurts out.

"Shhhh… what did I say! Don't act like it bothers you at all," comes Guy's command admonition.

"Oh, it doesn't bother me. I've seen all kinds in my short life. But this is just a bit much. I don't know if I can keep from laughing."

"Don't worry, laughing won't be a problem. At the right time. If you spend enough time with them, it won't be long before they try to make you laugh. Like I said, they're frigid people."

Guy steps in front of the group and greets the clown, Grimaldian, who appears to be their leader, "Hey there Squeaky! How are you my dear friend?"

"Ahhh, it's always such a huge pleasure when you return from your business trips. Who's this new friend?"

Guy turns and takes PhD's hand. "This is PhD. She's joined our business as a partner. Is she not a vision?"

"Not exactly my taste in humanoids. But based on your odd appearance, she seems an outstanding example of a female. Hello my dear. I'm Squeaky, leader of the Grimaldian people and protector of the Guy's home. At your service." He bows and a squeak sounds from beneath his garments.

PhD can no longer restrain a giggle as she bows in return. No squeak included.

"Ahhh, she has giggles. We'll get along just fine." Squeaky smiles, which causes his lips to droop downward in what most humanoids would consider a huge and frightening frown.

"What've you brought us from your travels Guys?"

Guy steps up to the crates and opens a couple. "We have balloons for making animals and fun shapes here. And over here," he reaches into the crate and draws his hand back with a dramatic flourish, "giant spiral lollipops!"

"Ohhh... Guys! You are truly givers of joy!" Squeaky picks up a lollipop and examines it as if it's a fine jewel.

Squeaky instructs his companions to take the crates back to their city.

He asks, "Guys, and the lovely PhD, will you be with us long? Shall we prepare a feast?"

"Sorry old friend. We have some financial wizardry for you to perform and then we must be off. Your offer is much appreciated and we'll make time for a feast soon," Guy replies.

"As you wish, your pleasure is our pleasure. Glad tidings to you all. Come with me and we'll take care of your financial needs," Squeaky replies and turns to follow the others. His feet making short squeak noises with each step.

"Certainly!" Guy replies. He follows him down the path to the city.

◊ ◊

PhD wanders over to the edge of the cliff that makes up the front porch. The floor is polished sparkling black granite and a railing has been carved from the natural rock. The view is awe inspiring. The gentle waves breaking over the various outcroppings of the volcanic rocks create an ever-changing tapestry. Her golden hair is picked up by the breeze and floats around her face and shoulders.

She reaches down to the belt of her activity suit

and dials it to a sexy, almost not there, sundress style. It, too, is now blowing in the breeze and exposing most of her luscious body.

Guy steps up to her side. "Just an amazing view isn't it?"

"Oh, my, yes. I don't see how you two even leave such a lovely home. I could spend endless days enjoying this."

"When you get a few hundred stanyears on you, you crave some action in your life, believe me."

"I suppose that would be true."

"Tell me about your friends the Grimaldians."

"A fascinating story. We stumbled upon this place while looking for somewhere to build our hideout. We had EVAC U8 doing searches on the galactic charts for Fly codes that were seldom, if ever, dialed. Most of them turned out to be dumps or dangerous places. Which is why they were so seldom dialed. Then we came here and were just shocked by what we found. The planet, the cavern system in the volcano and the greatest people.

"Oh, look!" Guy points toward the water as a massive school of rainbow colored fish breaches playfully in the surf.

PhD sighs.

"Turns out that the Grimaldians have a real problem with how people perceive them. They don't think they're funny looking at all. They get offended if someone laughs when they're not trying to make them laugh. So they keep pretty much to themselves.

"However, they have a unique thing going here. The star system really only has this one planet. The remaining mass in the system is made up of asteroids and a few planetoids. The asteroids are almost entirely water. As you know, water is a precious commodity in the galaxy. Especially among the highly developed and wasteful planets.

"The Grimaldians figured this out a couple of stancenturies back and decided to capitalize on it. They developed some amazing asteroid towing ships and started taking them through the Fly to other systems.

"The challenge of how they look and act was really getting to them. When they tried to socialize they were derided and ostracized by other more normal looking humanoids. Like there is such a thing. They decided they wanted nothing to do with any of them except business contact. And they wanted to keep their source of water and home world location a secret.

"When we first found them that was the problem they hadn't solved. They could get the ice to other systems without issues. The issue was having to take bizarre routes back through the Flies to keep from being followed or found out.

"We put EVAC on the problem. We knew that we couldn't access the Fly control systems directly. No one has ever managed to do that. However, EVAC discovered we could put a filter on their Fly that intercepted dialing signals. Can't control or change them, but can respond to them. If anyone other than they or us tries to dial this Fly, it responds with a dialing error message. It's a fake message. If someone were to dial and go through they'd get here. But the error message works like a charm. Now both the Grimaldians and we are safe from discovery."

"Amazing. And I can see how they'd be sensitive. My first impulse was to laugh when I saw them.

How awful to have that be everyone's reaction to meeting you."

"Worse than that. You'd be surprised how many people are terrified by clowns. They're profiled by the police and children run screaming. It's almost impossible for them to walk down a street without someone throwing something at them. Forget walking around after dark. It's clear cut racial prejudice. The Grimaldians were so grateful that we didn't treat them like freaks that they helped us build out our fantastic little home."

"What about Guy asking Squeaky for financial wizardry?"

"That talent is a byproduct of their desire to stay hidden. When huge sums of credits started rolling in from the ice business, they had to find a way to keep others from tracing them through the financial system.

"Squeaky's partner Snorty has an amazing talent for computer hacking. He's developed ways of making credits appear and disappear in the galactic accounting systems. I don't even begin to understand the complexity of it, and I majored in accounting. Well, one of the times I was in school anyway.

"When we get a payment from the Guild, or our other ventures, they make it disappear until we need it. When we need credits, they reappear in the right account at the right time. We've moved trillions of credits through the galaxy and, today, our account appears all but empty to anyone poking around. We look broke on any given day.

"The only downside to this is that we can't use the FlyCom to just make a transfer. That might be traceable. We have to come meet with them and make arrangements in advance. The transactions can't happen too quickly or too often."

"I can't get over how intricate and fascinating your lives are." PhD sighs. Then she leans against Guy's shoulder.

Guy is now in a state of glorious suspended animation.

◊ ◊

Down in the city, Guy and Squeaky are discussing some financial manipulations as they enter Squeaky's offices. Snorty, Squeaky's partner, is engrossed in intricate coding on a terminal. He jumps up when he realizes Guy is there.

"Guy! What a joy to have you with us! Are you staying long?"

"Hello my friend. It's always a pleasure to be with you! As always, your face buried in a terminal full of baffling code. Sadly, we're on a short layover. A longer and more relaxing visit is in our future." Guy smiles at the thought of that being true.

"Sad to hear, but still joyous in your presence!

"I feel the need for a stimulant drink before the markets open on Epsilon. Would either of you care for one?" Snorty grins an infatuated grin at Guy.

"No, thank you Snorty, I'm fine" replies Guy.

"I'll take one please."

Snorty then bows to them both, accompanied by a short snort, and makes his exit.

"Squeaky, what I need is to move one hundred million credits into active use. This big adventure we're wrapped up in may have some immediate costs. We may have to be gone for a while to get all of the pieces together and the deal closed. I don't want to have to worry about the balance on the public card."

"No problem Guy. We can get that started right away. Shouldn't take more than a few standays to get the various transfers done. Will that work for you?"

"Absolutely, you're the best! We're lucky to have such wonderful friends."

"Sorry to hear you'll be gone so long. It's always such a joy to have you with us.

"I have a few things here for you to approve." Squeaky points at a terminal nearby. "Just a quick finger print on this screen." Guy complies. "Then this one both here and here." Guy presses away. "One last one here for the Cheung Shipping Board of Directors votes."

Guy spends some time reviewing the Board actions and tapping his approval or rejection.

"That should do it for now." Squeaky touches a few pads and closes out the session.

"Squeaky, what would we do without you?"

"Guy, there's one other thing I need to talk to you about."

"You sound so serious old friend, what is it?"

"Someone from the Guild side tried to do a trace on their recent payment to you. They're pretty talented. Took us a bit of hard work to misdirect them and still keep the credits coming to the right accounts. We're monitoring it now. Don't use this account for a while until I know it is safe. We've setup a new account for your daily business." Squeaky hands him a card with the account information on it.

"Hmmm... now that's not good news. Andakosh and I go way back and I've always felt that, though he's shady, at heart he'd never cross us. After all, we saved his balls in a big way once."

"Sometimes a big adventure brings out the worst in a person. Is he involved in this new adventure of yours?"

"That's what's funniest. No, not yet anyway. We just made a delivery to him, that's the payment you saw being traced. He did act a little odd. Then we had to boost from Elttaes because some thug tried to steal Guy's crystal pendant necklace. Was not a pretty scene. I wonder if there's a connection?"

"Hard thing to know.

"I have Snorty working on hacking the hacker to find out what we can. I would council that you be much more cautious around Andakosh and the Guild in general for now. We can't be sure if it was him or someone in his organization going rogue."

"Good advice old friend, as always. Never think for a moment that we aren't grateful that our finances are in your capable hands. I need to scurry on back to the others and check on the status of the *Thrill*. We have a lot of work ahead of us."

"Guy, you should come home and rest sometime soon. You'll die young from your frantic work pace."

"You're too kind, and you're right. Soon my friend, we'll drink by the sea and tell stories. A promise!"

As Guy reaches the office door he pauses. "Oh grak! I almost forgot. Squeaky, can you send a payment of one million credits to a Director Mamang on Solipsismia for me? Notate as 'From the Guys. Payment for services rendered.' if you would."

"Certainly Guy. No problem."

Guy jogs back up the path to the front porch. He rounds the last bend and sees Guy with PhD resting on his shoulder. *This is going to be complicated.*

Threesomes are never easy.

"Hey! Enjoying the view?" he calls out.

PhD sighs and steps back from the railing of the porch. "Oh, Guy, this view is just overwhelming. So peaceful and beautiful. Too bad we have to leave. Please promise we'll be back again soon."

In unison, "You bet! You're a member of the family now!" The Guys speak in unison a lot.

◊ ◊

Back in the cavern, they wander onto the bridge of the *Thrill of Agony* to check in with EVAC U8.

Guy asks, "EVAC, how are we looking?"

"I can't say that you look any different. The MaintMechs have almost completed repairs on all the systems damaged of late. I'd say about another stanhour and we'll be clean and green. Uh, well, purple."

"Sounds perfect."

"There's one thing that disturbs me."

"What?"

"When Guy and I were running from the Guild, they managed to blow a hole in the cargo bay even though our shields were at full power. I analyzed the data from the attack. It seems the drone that nailed us was using the same trick we used to disable the *Portfolio*. It was modulating its weapons between plasma and pulse cannon shots focused on the same point on the ship. In addition, there's the slight lag in shield coverage when the ship is morphing that only made matters worse."

"Guy, I really wish you'd think twice before you flip people off with the ship." Guy is using his not happy about that command voice.

"OK... OK... you're right, I know." Guy is using his genuinely sorry command voice.

"I knew that trick was going to get figured out someday. Is there anything we can do about that?"

PhD interrupts, "Let EVAC and me work on this for a bit. Time for me to earn my rum. Isn't that a piratey thing?"

The Guys and EVAC U8 chuckle.

"I think I have a solution in mind."

"OK by us. I hear the mood elevator in the man cave calling our names."

Guy smiles and grabs Guy by the arm. They wander off to catch a buzz while PhD and EVAC U8 get to work.

"What you said is that you used modulated alternating plasma and energy pulses from the weapons to penetrate the *Portfolio's* shields?"

"Yes, it's a trick we figured out a while back. It causes the target's shield generators to constantly flip from one state to another. Eventually they overload from the effort and a shot gets through. A couple of volleys and we have a hole in the target."

PhD is now pulling up schematics and analysis on the holoskin screen in front of her. She spends some time working out equations on a holoboard and drawing up various circuit diagrams. She is focused and smiling. PhD is in her element now.

"So, EVAC my friend, what if we were to modify the lenticular modulation matrix system to do the same thing?"

"Your friend?"

"Oh, yes. You and I are going to be great friends!"

"Yes, of course we are. And yes, I see where you're going. If we phase the shield energy pattern in an overlapping matrix it might work."

"That's what I'm thinking. We create a multilayer shield net with each layer only modulated to one weapon type rather than a homogenous shield wave. Keep the frequencies tight enough and no manner of modulation on the enemy's part can make a coherent penetration.

"Since the different modulations for each layer of the shields will be steady-state, there's no overload on the generators from the phase switching.

"My simulations even show that the weakness during morphing will be reduced by at least half as the lag will be in different layers of the matrix at different times."

"That's pure genius! You're the most amazing humanoid I've been with since Cheung."

"Oh, really, it's just physics." She smiles a broad smile.

"I'll get the mechs to fabricate the necessary changes right away. This change will make the Guys happy and keep us all safer every time they stumble into trouble."

"Excellent! This has been fun. We're going to have a lot of great adventures together."

"Why don't you join the Guys and get some food. This shouldn't take more than two stanhours to complete."

"How nice of you EVAC. That's a splendid idea. Let us know when everything is shipshape." She giggles. "I just had to say that, sounds so piratey."

She wanders off the *Thrill of Agony* and joins the Guys. Guy opens up a magnificent view of the sea on one of the wall size holoskins. A large pod of enormous fish breaches and plays in the sparkling waves.

As they eat and make small talk, PhD fills the Guys in on the new feature, "You'll love what EVAC and I came up with."

"Really," both Guys at once, with food in their mouths.

"Boys, don't talk with your mouths full!"

"Smurry,"

"We're modifying how the *Thrill's* shields operate. The standard these days is to project a unified wave of shield energy that has to be modulated for each type of weapon hitting it. That puts a huge amount of stress on the generator systems.

What we came up with is a way to modulate the shields as a net in layers that are the inverse of the way you modulate weapons to disable the shields on your prey. The generators are running in a constant state, so no overload. In effect, when they use your trick against you, it won't work."

"That's excellent news!" Guy slaps Guy on the shoulder.

"No Doubt! You're going to make an outstanding pirate my dear. Our adventures will be made into a Sensie someday."

"Oh, Guy, I was just using my Sisterhood training." She's blushing.

"Nonsense! You have a natural gift!" interjects the other Guy.

While Guy is thinking, *Ohhh, yesss, I'm certain she has natural gifts.*

Guy receives the thought and just smiles at Guy wryly.

"Guys?" PhD has a mischievous smile. "I've never tried these mood elevators. In fact, I think I've been a bit too serious all my life. Can you show me what they're all about?"

The Guys choke back huge smiles. "Of Course!"

Guy explains, "You place your hand on this pad. The system runs a diagnostic and determines what mixture of mood altering goodies will elevate you to a happy state. It queries your brain patterns and metabolic makeup. You can then choose intravenous, pill, drink, smoke or any combination of those."

"Fascinating. Let's give it a try. I'm feeling freer than I've felt in my life right now. Let's have some fun!"

She places her hand on the pad and waits for the system to indicate analysis complete. She doesn't care much for smoking or injections so she chooses drink. The system dispenses a combination of Slur wine and a variety of biologic and chemical additives. She takes a large sip and the Guys pour another round of their current choice.

"It doesn't have an instantaneous effect, does it? Though, with my Sisterhood training, this may not work at all. Bottoms up, let's get some action." She drains her first glass and fills another, and another.

"Now, PhD, you should pace yourself."

Guy is feigning concern and hoping she gets sloshed. Would be way too much fun to see.

It's not long before PhD becomes animated. "You know, this is starting to feel good!"

Her arms waving and she's grinning from ear-to-ear in that animated way of speaking only the drunk can perform.

"We're going to have such great adventures Guys! This pirate stuff is SO not what I've done so far in my life." She gets up and starts dancing around the man cave looking at everything at random.

"Did you know I was top of my class in The Physics of Self Defense?"

"Really?"

"Yep, hold my goblet and watch this!"

Without hesitation, she launches into a back flip over the entertainment couch. She sticks the landing but then wobbles and knocks two game control modules off of a cart. To the Guys' astonishment, she catches both before they hit the floor. She spins, kicks and then places them back on the cart in what looks like one fluid movement.

Both Guys start clapping, Guy says, "Now that was well worth the price of admission. You keep telling us we're amazing. I think you have some amazing hiding in there as well."

She takes back her goblet from Guy, downs it and refills it. On one of the holoskin screens, the Guys had been watching one of the latest in the series *Humanoids Go Wild*. Women, men and whatever of all variation of humanoid are doing crazy things and losing their clothes.

PhD looks up and notices that the current episode is showing a wild party scene at a huge MES. A group of girls have pulled their tops down and are trying to balance their drink goblets on their ample breasts. Failing at every attempt.

"What amateurs! It's all just physics. Let me show you!" Pointing at the screen.

With that, she pulls down the top of her dress and lets it hang from the belt. She takes her goblet, considers various angles and does a few quick test rests. She adjusts her posture and places the goblet balanced on her left breast.

"See, no so shard!" She wobbles a bit and some spills. "Guy, gib me yours, anybody can do just one!"

Guy hands up his goblet while Guy just sits in mesmerized delirium. She takes Guy's goblet and balances it on her right breast.

"BAM! Snailed it!" She grabs both goblets and takes another big gulp of hers. She hands Guy his back and refills hers.

She starts singing, "YO HO HO it's pirates we be! Off on fantastic adventures, just we three! "

She's now spinning around like a little girl on a lark. Her dress twirling around her, arms and perfect breast spinning out from her like a carnival ride. Always true to her Sisterhood training, she's demonstrating the effects of centripetal force.

EVAC U8 comes over the comport, "The modifications to the shields succeeded. All simulations show stable operation. We're ready to boost whenever you are.

"That PhD is an amazing addition to the crew."

PhD laughs and announces, "Well Wooo Weee!"

"PhD, are you all right?"

"Hime Fine-eeo EVAC ol' budgy! Well Guys, you heard my budgy. The ship is fix-eeo so let's boost-eeo to Angs... Angstuh... Oh, letz go find out about our crystal-eeos."

With that, she raises her glass and laughs.

Guy steadies her and takes her back to a couch. "Here, put your hand on the pad again. It'll generate a cleansing drink. You'll be back to sober in stanseconds."

She wobbles her hand to the pad. Takes the drink and downs it in one long gulp. The Guys just stare in rapt lewd thoughts, which they won't be sharing.

They head for the *Thrill of Agony* and PhD is transitioning from a stumble drunk zig zag walk to a fashion model runway walk. By the time they board the ship, she's dialed her Dial-Your-Style to a sexy feminine version of the Guys' pirate activity suits. A better look on her than they. She's now sober and clear eyed.

The Guys just look at each other. Both thinking, *Are we not the luckiest pirates in the galaxy!*

◊ ◊

Everyone is tinkering with this and that system in that usual flurry of switching switches and pressing buttons that goes on to get ready to boost.

PhD's eyes light up. "Guys, it dawns on me. If I'm going to join the amazing crew of the *Thrill of Agony*, don't you think I should be trained on how to operate her?"

The Guys look at each other, the stress of thinking showing on their faces. Guy nods to Guy.

"I think that's a fantastic idea. If you're taking up a couch, might as well get some use out of you." He chuckles.

Guy hits the comport. "Squeaky?"

"Yes, Guy."

"We're getting ready to head out. We're going to give PhD some driving lessons before we leave the system. Don't freak out if you see the *Thrill* flying around and shooting at a few asteroids. OK?"

"No problem Guy. Good luck PhD!"

"Everyone couch-up. School is now in session."

Guy and PhD chuckle as they slide into their couches and prepare for takeoff.

"Lesson one. Getting out of The Circus without breaking anything."

"Change the couch configuration to 'Command' on the list on the left. Hit the pad marked 'Prep for Takeoff' and check that the *Thrill* clears all systems. Green lights across the board."

"Got it!" PhD is excited.

"VENTI L8. Feel free to override if anything goes

south, otherwise, PhD has the helm."

"Ready Guy. She'll do just fine."

"Put your favorite steering hand on the control orb and press the thrust selector pad to engage Landing Thrusters.

Guy interjects, "Later, if you want, you can change out the control orb for the antique joystick style. I prefer it myself. I have mine customized. It has a chrome shaft with a black ebony skull on the top."

"You're such a boy." PhD chuckles.

The *Thrill of Agony* lifts off the floor of the cavern and is floating a stanmeter off the floor.

"Excellent. Now swing the *Thrill* around to face the doors and take her forward."

"This isn't so hard." PhD smiles. Then clang and crash, one of the landing struts clips a tool cart.

"OK, no major damage. Doing fine. Now that we're clear of the doors, set the thrust selector to Main Impulse. Be careful at first, the *Thrill* is built for speed."

PhD sets the selector and then pushes down on the chrome foot gas pedal. The *Thrill of Agony* lurches forward pressing them all deep into their couches.

She lets off. "OH! Sorry about that. Controls are touchy aren't they?"

"OK, just head out to open space. Do some swooping around and get a feel for things for a few stanminutes."

PhD floors it again. They streak toward space with a trail of vapor and a sonic boom everyone could hear. She does a series of barrel rolls, figure eights and loops. The Guys are staring at each other with more than a little surprise showing on their faces, and holding on to their couches.

"PhD, you need to get a handle on battle maneuvers. A ship like this doesn't turn instantly. You have to anticipate your moves. Take a swipe at an asteroid. The goal is to get close but not hit it."

"OK"

She aims the *Thrill of Agony* at a nearby asteroid and floors it. She comes in hot and, as she goes to make the turn, she's coming in too hot. In the last stansecond before the *Thrill of Agony* will hit the asteroid, EVAC U8 takes the helm. The shields activate and they brush the asteroid with a puff of debris and a hard bounce.

"OH SHIT! Sorry about that. Thanks EVAC!"

"No worries. You aren't the only humanoid on the bridge who has needed my help to avoid crashing."

"OK, that was fun. Time to try an axis flip PhD. You'll see a yellow pad next to the orb labeled 'Hang On'. See it?"

"Yes, but really, labeled Hang On?"

"You'll understand. When you want to do an axis flip you level out the ship first. Then when you hit that pad, two of the main impulse engines rotate ninety degrees and fire. Flips the ship over. It's a fantastic maneuver during battle and the only way to stop and reverse the ship once she's going any speed at all. Give it a try, but heed the warning."

PhD hits the pad and everyone is crushed into their couches once again.

After a moment of disorientation. "SHIT! That was cool. That'll come in handy."

"Ohhh... Kaaa... PhD, looks like you have that down. Let's look for something to shoot at.

"RUMIN-8? Do we have an asteroid convenient

to our current location?"

"Checking… yes, setting course for you PhD."

"Thanks EVAC!"

"Let's change your couch configuration to Weapons Control. That's the third seat job we can use the most right now. Given how often we seem to be shooting, and being shot at, lately.

"Guy, you take helm and make some attack runs at the asteroid for her."

"Ready"

"PhD, on your console you should see a large selection of weapons and a targeting control display."

"No shit! I had no idea the *Thrill of Agony* even carried so many weapons. I didn't notice them when I was admiring her."

"More than half the weapons on the *Thrill* are hidden. Gives us an edge." Guy smiles.

"We won't worry about everything at once. Just select cannon systems and a joystick should pop out of the arm of your couch. Guy will make some wild swings around the asteroid. Center it up in the targeting circle. Then fire at will. Your job is not missing. Easy!" Guy grins.

In no time at all, the asteroid is covered in small blast craters.

Guy is impressed. "PhD you're a natural. I've never seen anyone take to this like you are. You have awesome instincts."

Guy adds, "Just to round things out. You'll see selector pads that let you choose which weapons are controlled by your stick. The default you just used selects the guns based on your target. You can link just one to your joystick and set any or all of the others to track a target and lay down constant fire. You can link them all to your joystick. And you can just set the system to establish a sphere of defense. That setting assigns a gun to every angle of approach and shoots anything that moves.

"You'll also see pads to select one of three types of torpedoes we carry; tranquilizer, lurking and standard. You've already seen how lurking works. Standard does what you'd expect, pick a target and fire. The tranquilizer is what you saw us use on the *Portfolio*. The blue gas that knocks everyone out."

Guy interjects, "Don't be too concerned at first. VEGET-8 can also run the weapons systems for you if things get too intense. Just tell him what you want to do and he'll figure out what to shoot when."

PhD grins as she examines the options on her console. "This is amazing. The *Thrill* is a sleek and ominous galactic cruiser!"

Guy gets serious for a moment, "There's one last critical feature we need to show you. We've only used it once, just to test it. If you're going to fly the *Thrill*, you have to know how to scuttle her."

"Scuttle her?" PhD looks concerned.

"The *Thrill of Agony* has a Lifeboat Mode. Something you need to understand but hope you never have to use. When activated, it morphs the bridge into a shuttle craft and separates from the rest of the ship. The rest of the ship just continues on doing whatever it was doing at that moment. If we're lucky, you've saved our lives from some horrible death.

"First we have to get you paired with the system. On the upper right of your main console there's a small red door with a thumbprint reader below it. You need to stand up on one foot. Then place your right thumb on the pad and your left thumb on your nose. Spin around to the right…"

EVAC U8 interrupts, "Guy, very funny. PhD, I paired you with the system as soon as you put your thumb on the pad."

"YOU GUYS!"

"OK... OK..." Both Guys laughing so hard they're having trouble catching their breath.

"Let's move on. In all seriousness, this next part is no joke. Press your thumb on the pad and the door will open."

She does as instructed. There's a small red lever under the door. Printed down the lever are the words 'Are You SURE?' in space-glo safety yellow.

"Do NOT pull that lever right now. Trust us, it's not something you want to do for fun. A phall of a mess putting the ship back together after we tried it."

Guy adds, "Just so you know it's there. With some of the action we're seeing lately, you need to be able to save yourself, or all of us, if the ship takes a big one up the exhaust."

EVAC U8 adds, "PhD, my core is included in the lifeboat. However, my functionality will be limited. We will be separated from the majority of the *Thrill* and its systems. The lifeboat does have light armament and shields for defense."

PhD looks sad. "That part wasn't much fun, but I have it. We won't need it so no worries."

"OK, you've covered the basics. You'll get plenty of practice soon enough. Let's head for the Nervosis system. PhD, why don't you take us through the Fly."

– Seven –

In the Mucusan system, aboard the Pan-Man-Poo shuttle, Piobar sees the Fly closing after the *Thrill of Agony* makes its transit. The Fly status shows 'Available'. He makes his final settings and commences to dial the Fly for the Earth system.

He thinks, *I'm glad to be out of the constant danger those Guys seem to stumble into. They're a menace to the galaxy. I'll be much safer now.*

After a few stanseconds, nothing seems to be happening. He tries again. On the Fly Control Console a message appears, 'The Fly You Are Dialing Is Temporarily Out Of Service. Please Try Again At Some Unknown Time In The Future. Thank You.'

Piobar is now discovering what happens when a Pan-Man-Poo destroyer rams into a Hyperspace Fly. It's still off line. A good thing for the Guys and PhD, not so much for Piobar.

"Well SHIT! That's just dandy. Par for the course lately," he sighs.

He looks out the view ports at the beautiful expanse of space. "This is a lovely spot. I guess I'll go enjoy some fine Pan-Man-Poo autocuisine and relax."

He then realizes he's talking to himself and smiles. He thinks, *Perhaps I'll just lose my mind and none of this will any longer matter.*

He heads to the Officer's Mess to relax, eat and

drink his sorrows away. He decides to sample a little of everything. One thing leads to another and he's now several bottles of fine California wine into the gluttony.

"This has been so much fun, let's do it again. What do you think Doctor? I think that's a grand idea Doctor!" He's now talking to himself in a grand drunken delusion. Which seems to be working just fine, until he passes out across an entertainment couch.

He wakes up stanhours later in the entertainment couch listening to the most depressing classical music the ship has to offer. His head pounding and feeling like he's been beaten. He stumbles to the instashower and drinks a large mug of strong coffee to clear his head.

Head clearer, he hatches his plan, *Enough of this denial. I need to get back to Earth and rebuild my life. Oh, but wait. I can't just come flying in on this stolen shuttle. What to do? What do do?*

Ahhh... I'll go to Proxima and ditch the shuttle. Then take public transport back to Earth. They'll never know I was gone. Good plan.

To his surprise, the Fly control notifies him that the Fly is opening. He rushes back to the control center to assess the situation only to realize that the controls are showing an incoming ship, not his dial to Earth being completed. He also doesn't yet realize that he never moved his shuttle out of the Fly approach path.

He stands staring out the viewport wondering who might be coming along. A Helrisien light attack cruiser blasts through the Fly and passes within stanmeters of Piobar's shuttle.

He's so startled, and angry, he hits the comport

button without thinking. He presses his face through the holoskin display such that, on the Helrisien ship, it looks like his face is bulging in toward them.

Spittle flying from his mouth, he yells, "Whomever you are, be more carful will you! You almost crashed into my ship. Have a little respect for other ships!"

The Helrisien ship makes a sweeping U-turn and heads straight for him. He's so taken aback he stands frozen in front of the holoskin screen watching the fast approaching ship.

Aboard the Helrisien ship, the Captain is shouting, "That's the missing Consultant shuttle. I know that face. He's the old fool from the vid Slit sent us. The one who stole the shuttle. Lock onto that ship and prepare to board!"

Too quick for Piobar to even think of what to do, they're locked on and boarding. He thinks, *Damn! Where are those Guys when I need them!*

The Helrisien boarding party storms the bridge with weapons drawn.

The Captain barks, "Where are the others! Stand still or you'll be bleeding out where you fall! Team! Search the ship for the others."

Piobar rapid fire stutters, "But... But... that won't be necessary. I assure you I'm quite alone here. I have no idea who you're looking for. I'm just a scientist returning from a research mission. The Fly for the Earth system is malfunctioning or I'd be home by now. Can't we all calm down?"

"You were with the pirates. Don't try to lie to me old fat man!"

"You must be mistaken. I've been here for stanweeks doing medical research. I don't even enjoy having other beings around. Can't you tell by the depressing music I'm playing?"

"That's the first truth you've provided. Your music choice is pathetic. But I have no patience for deception and you'll start losing body parts soon. I like to start with fingers on fat old men. They're so tasty when deep fried. Your pudgy fingers look like a nice snack to me right now."

"I assure you, kind sir, I have nothing to offer on this subject. I'm at a loss as to how I can possibly help you."

"I need my favorite plot contrivance. Get me the Nerple device. On the double!"

"Sir, you do realize you have forcefully boarded a ship of the Pan-Man-Poo. This won't go well for you. I'm willing to forget this error if you just leave peacefully now." Piobar is trying bravado.

"Right, you're a Consultant and I'm a Farlaph Beast. You stole this ship anyway. Perhaps I should contact the Pan-Man-Poo and see what they think?"

Bluff called, nowhere to hide! Piobar is thinking as sweat is breaking on his brow.

A few moments later, one of the team of assassins returns with a piece of equipment that looks like a defibrillator.

"Do you know how this works?"

"Well, uh, no. Can you explain it? In great and lengthy detail perhaps?"

"Enough babbling! Grab him boys!" The Captain's face is hardening like concrete on a hot day.

With that, a couple of muscular and ugly thugs grab Piobar and throw him into a control couch. They rip his shirt open and proceed to attach leads from the device to his nipples.

"One last chance. Where are your friends?"

"I'd hardly call anyone a friend. Did you not catch that I'm a scientist? Who would want to hang out with someone as boring as myself? I mean really?" His stalling is useless, but he has to try.

"Give him the one setting just to show him what he has to look forward to."

One of the thugs presses a few buttons on the device and Piobar gets a look on his face that can only be describes as pleasureful pain.

"Seriously? You have no idea how boring my life is. That's the closest thing to sex I've had in a decade. Can you do it again?"

"Oh, a smartass are we? Try this!" He grabs the control and dials it to seven.

Piobar jerks about on the couch and starts to drool. Eyes as wide open as they can get. Unable to catch his breath to even scream. His pants are soaking wet.

He turns the device off and stands laughing at Piobar. "Is that more like your idea of a sex life?"

"Urgh... grumph... eeenoughhhh," is all the Doctor can get out. A huge stream of mucus running down his face and onto his chest like a waterfall.

"Now, that's better." He's smiling at the sight of his handy work. "Where do I find the people who attacked the Pan-Man-Poo?"

"Ugh... sniffle... they're on a ship named *Thrill of Agony*. The last place I knew they were headed is Angstuvia in the Nervosis system. I have no idea if they're still there. They don't stay in one place very long."

I've just sold out my companions. He winces as the thought flashes through his battered mind.

"Thank you so much. Would you like another jolt for the road?"

"NO! Please, NO!" Piobar is slumped in the control couch.

"Men! Back to the ship. We have our destination."

They march off the shuttle. All Piobar can do is watch in horror and think about the terrible fate that awaits the Guys and PhD. *Please let them be gone by the time these assholes arrive.*

Aboard the Helrisien vessel, the Captain makes certain our heroes won't be warned. "Gunner! Fire a low energy blast into that ships FlyCom deep space communication array. That'll keep that old fool from warning the pirates."

The Helrisien ship then activates the Fly and blasts away with a scream no one heard.

Piobar realizes he might have a chance to warn the Guys and PhD so he tries to dial the FlyCom to contact the *Thrill of Agony*. Across the holoskin a flashing red alert shows 'FlyCom Damaged. System Critical. Service Discounts Available At a Dealer Near You.'

Doctor Piobar collapses into the, now soaking wet, control couch and whimpers like a child. He breathes deeply through his nose. Then realizes he just breathed deeply through his nose.

He thinks, *Hmmm... the Anosmians are gone, odd.*

On the Helrisien ship, the Captain is contacting the Pan-Man-Poo.

"This is Cameron. What do you have to report Captain?"

"We missed the pirates but found the old fat man who stole your shuttle. By the way, he'll be coming your way soon."

"Thanks, we'll deal with him."

"We interrogated him and he gave us the intel we needed. They're on a ship named *Thrill of Agony*. They're heading to Angstuvia in the Nervosis system."

"Excellent, stay on their trail. Remember, this is a capture NOT kill mission. I'll inform The Partner. Cameron Out."

Supreme Commander Cameron then heads to The Partner's office. This time with a snap in his step and a little less concerned for his life. Not only is the Earth Hyperspace Fly back online, he has success in locating the attackers.

The Partner is just finishing up a conference call with one of the advance teams that had been out of contact for the last few days due to the Fly damage.

"Good. You've established their lack of ability to manage their world to the point that they mistrust even their own advisors. The opening we need to insinuate ourselves into the core of their government.

"Make sure you keep the pressure on their military leaders up by undermining the leadership council's confidence. We need the military under our control ASAP. Keep the Helrisien's engaged in threats against their ships and cities.

"Tell them not to overdo it, we don't want to lose any valuable assets. Just make the military look ineffective.

"Update me when you have control of their military. And keep your fee percentage high. The quarterly reports are due soon and I want to see all numbers up. That's all for now." He turns off the screen and turns toward Cameron.

"Sir, do you have a moment?" Cameron is still taking baby steps.

"Yes. Do you have an update on that foolish pirate who attacked the *Portfolio* yet?"

"Yes, sir. Our Helrisien team found and interrogated the old fool Doctor Piobar and have identified the ship and the occupants. They have intel on where they're headed next."

"Most excellent. They'll be in our hands soon then, correct? Don't think you're out of hot water yet Cameron. This is a HUGE debacle. Send one of our destroyers from the area to assist. If the Helrisiens mess this up, I want backup. They're thugs and I don't want any mistakes. We need to make a public example of those fools who dared attack us. Understood!"

"Yes, sir. I'll order a ship to join them immediately."

He receives a subcutaneous communication, *Sir, we have another raid by the pirates! This time on our ship in the Ulgvar system.*

"Well, shit! Let me transfer you to The Partner's holoskin."

The image of the reporting officer appears, "Go ahead Lieutenant."

"Yes, sirs. As I was saying, we had another raid. This time on our ship in the Ulgvar system. The raiding ship was one of our new shuttles. They just lined up with the other shuttles and were loaded with supplies before anyone realized what was going on. They destroyed a LoadMech and the Load Master was sucked out into space when they made their escape.

"One of our own transport ships swooped in, scooped them up and disappeared. We're at a loss to explain why one of our own would be stealing from us.

"No other casualties and the ship is being re-paired now. Here is the surveillance vid of the last moments of the raid."

As the vid comes up, The Partner's face turns bright red. "THAT FOOL! That's the same pirate who hit the *Portfolio*. What's going on? Is this raid the Pan-Man-Poo month and no one told me!

"Actually, that was a pretty crafty plan, now that I think about it. I'm beginning to think we aren't dealing with the run-of-the-mill idiot pirate scum. Using one of our shuttles and somehow, now, they have one of our ships. This crew seems to have skills. Too bad they're going to suffer and die by my hands.

"Make no mistake, Cameron, your career and op-tion grant package are being dangled over a fire right now. Bring an end to this thievery. Rumors are starting to spread and I will NOT have anyone doubting my greatness. Do not disappoint me! OUT!" The Partner makes an exaggerated point at the door and turns his back on Cameron.

There's panic on Cameron's face. He thinks, *This is out of control and I can feel The Partner's fist grip-ping my balls.*

◊ ◊

The *Thrill of Agony* now approaches the planets of the Nervosis system. Everyone is excited by the prospect of unraveling a lifelong mystery.

"Boys, can you believe we've had these crystals all this time and had no idea what they are? How powerful and dangerous they are?" PhD strokes her crystal and stares out the forward view port.

Guy is transfixed by the sight of PhD stroking her crystal so Guy decides to sound sincere, "Why would our parents give us something so powerful and yet give us no idea of the what, why and how?

"I wonder if knowing what they're capable of is the dangerous aspect of the crystals. I mean, let's face it, if they give you super powers it would be a huge temptation to use them in some bad ways."

EVAC U8 interrupts, "We're thirty stanminutes from Angstuvia."

PhD responds, "Thank you EVAC U8."

"Not at all. I'm at your service." EVAC U8 has a crew member who appreciates him and it shows in his demeanor.

She continues, "EVAC? Can you give us some background on the system and the planet we'll be visiting? I'm afraid I know a great deal more about the physics of the galaxy than the actual planets and civilizations."

"Certainly. There are three habitable planets in the Nervosis system. The first world is Angstuvia and our current destination. The most intellectually and economically advanced of the three planets by far.

"The second world is Phearallis. It's not as developed or economically prosperous as Angstuvia. Still a generally pleasant and prosperous planet intentionally held back by the powers of Angstuvia.

"The third world is Desperatis and is the least developed economically having been exploited by the other two worlds for stanmillennia. Desperatis is a rugged combination of jungle and arid mountains. It's mined and harvested without regard for the horrific environmental impact.

"They're even further exploited by major corporations that use their elderly citizens as slaves in call centers.

"The city we will be visiting, Paniclateris, is the

only city on Angstuvia. It occupies the entire equator of the planet for a distance of less than one hundred stankilometers outward from the equator."

"How fascinating. Why is that EVAC?"

"Angstuvia is the most advanced of the planets. They gained that status by exploiting the planet's resources and those of the other planets. Finally, Angstuvia was becoming uninhabitable for humanoid life and they panicked. They'd made no preparations or attempts to accept the reality of what they'd done. Their scientists fought with the various political and religious factions for stancenturies to no avail.

"By the time everyone accepted reality, they had but one option remaining. It was impossible to naturally reverse the global climate change cycle they'd created. In another hundred stanyears the atmosphere would have just burned off. They devised a last hope plan to cool the planet using geoengineering. They developed specifications for an elaborate system of projectors to reduce the atmospheric temperature.

"The obscenely wealthy controlling one percent of the planet's population balked at the extreme cost of building the system on Angstuvia. They felt the lower classes should carry the cost burden since there were more of them to benefit.

"The lower classes felt they would be unfairly burdened so they insisted that the work be outsourced to the second world, where costs are lower.

"The second world then outsourced the work to the third world and made a tidy profit as middlemen.

"The team managing the construction failed to

realize a minor, but critical, difference. The first world uses a system of measures that's based upon ancient aristocratic standards such as the length of the King's thumb. The third world, on the other hand, uses the Galactic Standard Measure system, as we do.

"When the geoengineering system was completed and installed, things went wrong fast. Angstuvia went from about to boil over to being almost entirely covered in a frozen wasteland. They managed to correct and stabilize the system but, by then, only a small band around the equator remained unfrozen and habitable.

"On the plus side, I suppose, Paniclateris does have temperate weather and it almost never rains in the city. The combination of wonderful climate in the city and immediate access to a frozen wonderland makes it a popular tourist destination for beings across the galaxy.

"Is that sufficient?"

PhD has an incredulous look on her face. "Uh... Yes, thank you EVAC. An excellent summary."

EVAC U8 updates the status, "We have clearance to land and I have us on vector to arrive in two stan-minutes."

"Guys, I think we should lose our pirate look. Go with something more touristy." PhD is a planner.

"Good idea!" comes their simultaneous reply. "How about this?"

They press a few buttons on the sashes of their pirate activity suits and their Dial-Your-Style changes into flowered shirts and baggy shorts.

"Perfect!" PhD smiles and dials her garment to a flowing flowered dress. "Oh, and we should put the crystals out of sight."

As they deship, over their shoulders the scrolling sign board on the *Thrill* has changed. It now reads 'Ski season is at its peak in the Western Hemisphere. Discount passes available from many fine ski retailers...'

They stroll up to the entry office and ask for directions to shopping information. They're told there's a Tourist Info Monolith just a few stanmeters from the fountain in the main plaza. And off they go.

The plaza is almost overwhelming to behold. Green and lush with the most amazing fountain in the center. The fountain sprays water in mesmerizing dancing patterns, occasionally reaching a stankilometer in the air. The water from the highest sprays vaporizes and becomes beautiful puffy clouds.

There's an immense aquarium several stories tall and blocks long that's on their left as they stroll into the plaza. They stop to admire the wide variety of fish and other sea life swimming about. A large eel darts out of some coral outcroppings and grabs a small fish.

PhD jumps behind Guy and screams, "An eel!"

Guy turns around and puts his hands on her shoulders. "Calm down PhD. It's just a fish in a box. It can't get you out here."

"What's up with the eel fear anyway?" Guy asks.

"When I was a teenager, my father taught me to SCUBA dive. We had many great adventures together.

"Then on one trip, a giant eel came out of nowhere and grabbed my dad's leg. I beat the eel off of him with my flashlight and we had to rush him to the hospital. There was blood everywhere. Ever since, even the mention of eels makes my blood curdle. I want nothing to do with them, ever!"

Guy sees a change of subject is needed. "There it is." Pointing at the monolith ahead and to their right.

They turn to head that direction. A hand grabs the other Guy by the shoulder and spins him around. Before anyone can blink, Guy has drawn his plasmascimitar from his baggy shorts pocket. He presses the hilt into the abdomen of his assailant and pauses before activating it.

"HOLD IT GUY! Calm down. It's just me, Lucridius, old friend."

Guy stares into his face. "Give me one reason I shouldn't close my grip and puncture you like one of those silly balloons over there?" Pressing the hilt harder into Lucridius' abdomen.

"Oh, come on, you can't still be mad about that 3D-poker game on Laswagius can you? You know we were both trying to cheat the fat orange-skinned freak with the loud mouth and small brain."

Guy growls, "As I remember, you ended up with all the profit and I had to fight my way out of there when he called in his body guards."

"OK, true enough. But you have to admit, we had one phall of a good time!" Lucridius is now smiling that knowing smile of a conspirator.

"I think you had a bit more fun than I did. I had to spend a stanweek hustling enough to pay off my margin at the casino." Guy is giving up his anger to the memories of all the other fun the two had there. He returns his plasmascimitar to his pants.

"What brings you Guys and... phlurg!... this complete angel of my wildest desires to Paniclateris?"

"Since you appear to be a friend of Guy's, you may call me PhD. But do not think you have the right to take any liberties with me!" PhD is making the sign of the Sisterhood again.

"Oh, I see. You're a Disciple of the Sisterhood. I didn't realize. My apologies. But you know you're a vision of beauty." Lucridius was not about to let up on the flirting.

"That's true, and beside the point sir." PhD turns away to look at the fountain.

Guy thinks, *Wow, never thought I'd see her take such an instant dislike to someone. Although, have to admit, she's judged his character pretty spot on.*

The Guys stand with Lucridius for a moment. "We're here to do some shopping and relax a bit. Our lovely companion has a thing for exotic crystals. We have a thing for excessive mood elevation. From what we hear, this is the place for us."

"Indeed it is! There are some amazing live pornie shows and they serve a fabulous buffet at lunch time. Drinks are expensive, but you can't beat the shapeshifting dancing girls. Whew, can they turn a head or two!"

"Excellent, we'll have to look into those later. First we need to show off our charm to PhD and help her shop for crystals. Any ideas?

"Not exactly something I spend time thinking about, sorry."

"She likes those quaint little shops off the main tourist path. Says they have the most unique goods. She mentioned one called A Penchant for Crystals, if I remember correctly."

"As a matter of fact, there's an app for that." He points to the monolith just a few steps away. "Let's look it up."

They step up to the monolith and Lucridius inputs 'penchant for crystals'. A map appears.

"Looks like the shop is just a few blocks south of the hypertube station at 6608099th Street East. Whew, that's a fair distance away. That's your ride." He points over their shoulders to the sleek elevated tube running through the city.

"That was easy. Thanks old friend." Guy slaps Lucridius on the back, a bit harder than required.

"No problem Guy." Lucridius regains his footing. "Do watch yourselves out there. It's off the main tourist routes in an old part of the city."

"True that old friend. We'll keep ourselves in line. Thanks so much for the tip. Let's get together this evening for some drinks." Guy is using another of his endless supply of command lies.

"Sounds great. There's a mood elevation station called the Angry Orbit. Ask anyone, it's popular. No need to rush, I'll be there all evening anyway." Lucridius is beaming at the idea of spending time with PhD. His mistake.

PhD rejoins the conversation just in time to hear this. "Thank you for your assistance. Maybe you aren't such a bad sort." Once again using her voice control techniques and mixing in her first official command lie.

She Thinks, *I just told a lie! I think I enjoyed it!*

She may be good for the Guys, but they're rubbing off on her. She can't help but smile a smile so disarming that none of the gents would care if she lied to them all night long.

They part ways with Lucridius and head for the hypertube station. Not realizing they're being observed by a group of four rather angry looking men in business suits. Their suits and ties loosened so as to appear to be tourists. A failed attempt. It's hard for a Consultant to blend into anything that resembles relaxed.

The Consultants start to follow our heroes as they head for the hypertube. Lucridius notices this. In a rare act of character, he heads to intercept them. Along the way, he grabs a bunch of large colorful floating bird balloons from a distracted street vendor's cart. He rushes up to the four Consultants.

"Hey, you folks look like you need some color in your lives. Aren't you here to relax?" Lucridius is talking fast and walking around them in circles.

"Balloons are only three credits. Bet a balloon like this might even get you lucky with a lady." He thrusts a giant four-winged bird balloon in the face of the Consultant closest to him.

In all the confusion, our trio has disappeared into the crowd. The Consultants push Lucridius out of the way and scan the crowded plaza. A look of despair crosses their faces. The lead Consultant reaches up to his neck and activates his subcutaneous comport.

Lucridius slinks away into the crowd letting the balloons float away in the breeze. He thinks, *That should do it. They won't catch up to them anytime soon. Time for a drink and a few good fantasies involving that Disciple babe.*

The lead Consultant subvocalizes, "Message for the Commander. We spotted the pirates on Angstuvia. Lost them in the crowd. Continuing to pursue."

The Guys and PhD whoosh along in the hypertube car looking at the sites of the city. PhD gets a quizzical look on her face.

"What are you thinking about my lovely?" Guy wonders.

"I was just thinking about the street the shop is on." She pulls out her pocket holoskin. "Look at this." She writes down the number on the holoskin.

"Ok, it's a big number. It's a really really big city." Guy is confused.

"Watch..." She turns the holoskin 180 degrees so the number is upside down. "It's the same number. It's called a strobogrammatic prime. They're rare and it's more than a little interesting that the shop we seek is on a street with that number."

"Interesting." Guy shrugs. "Oh, look, here we are."

They arrive at the 6608099th Street East hyper-tube station and detube in the direction the map showed. They stroll down the street looking for the shop.

PhD comments, "You know, for a city this immense, they really keep things tidy. This is an old part of the city and it doesn't appear too rough at all."

She then stops with an almost earie gleam in her eyes. "Guys, I think something is wrong. I feel like we're in danger."

The sound of heavy footsteps erupts behind the group. Guy wheels around to see what's going on. Coming at them in a hurry are two Helrisien thugs. And they look focused.

Guy nudges Guy. "Looks like we have unwanted guests on our little stroll."

"Oh, those animals again. Never seem to get enough of them do we." Guy is half smug and half scared.

The Guys step in front of PhD and draw their plasmascimitars. The impression plasmascimitars make is always interesting. Nothing else like them in the galaxy. The two thugs slow down from the surprise of seeing the plasmascimitars, then continue to approach.

One thug looks at the other and says, "Looks like we might have to take them back to the Captain a little damaged." He laughs and lunges.

PhD steps to the side and leaps forward. Using her Disciple training in the art of physics and self-defense, she ducks under the first thug's wild swing and uses the momentum of his lunge to send him flying into a nearby fire hydrant. He lands with the hydrant planted in the middle of his back. He flops once and he's done. One thug that won't be home for dinner.

While this is happening, the Guys have engaged the second thug. In a badly choreographed mess of bumping into each other, they manage to slice off two of his arms.

He draws his side blaster with another arm and Guy deflects the shot with his plasmascimitar while Guy slices off that arm. The thug stumbles, recovers and presses the attack once again using a large commando knife and his only remaining arm.

"GRAK! These thugs just don't know when to quit!"

Guy is dancing on Guy's feet as he moves to finish the fight. Guy turns his back on the Helrisien, locks his hands in front of him to make a stirrup, then Guy steps up on Guy's hands and Guy launches Guy into a perfect somersault over the thugs head.

Guy slices his plasmascimitar through the thug's neck. A cut so clean that his head bobbles before falling off his shoulders. The head lands on the pavement rolling up to PhD's feet. The remainder of the Helrisien lunges on from pure adrenaline. He takes several stumbling steps and then falls at Guy's feet.

The head looks sideways up at PhD and tries to bite her foot.

"OK, remind me to avoid these animals," she says, dusting her hands and kicking the head toward the nearby dumpster.

The Guys take the other remnants of the thugs and toss them into the dumpster. "Filjab! These Helrisiens are heavy."

"What the hell was all that about?" PhD is sounding nervous.

"No idea. We cross, double and triple cross a lot of folks in the course of a workday. Hard to say which we did to these two. Either way, we need to keep moving. Helrisiens travel in packs and they'll have a nasty ship nearby as well." Guy is scanning up and down the street.

Guy has to comment, "PhD my dear, you're just a beautiful bundle of surprises. Those moves of yours are spectacular. How did you know that was about to happen?"

"Oh, the fighting technique is nothing, just physics," she smiles. "I guess I never mentioned it before. I'm an empath. I can't see the future or anything as useful as the winning lottery numbers. It's more that I pick up feelings and see patterns.

"When those thugs got ready to attack, their emotions bubbled up and I picked up the vibe of danger. Not as useful as it sounds, but comes in handy occasionally.

"Now those swords of yours, those are something that comes in handy."

As they turn back to their work of finding the crystal shop, they almost knock down an elderly man coming out of, what else, the crystal shop.

"Ugh! Watch where you're going!" he says, in a voice full of gravel.

What's up with people's voices? Geez, now this old man sounds like he has a mouth full of gravel? PhD is perplexed.

PhD looks up above his head and sees the sign 'A Penchant for Crystals' over the shop door. "Excuse me sir. We're so sorry. We're just in a hurry to find this shop."

"What do you want in my shop? I'm about to head to lun..." He doesn't finish the sentence as he sees the crystal that's come loose from between PhD's breasts during the fight. He starts to reach out to it. With a look of frightened remembrance he pulls his hand back.

PhD quickly nestles her crystal back in its hiding place.

"Please, where are my manners. Business is business and business has been slow. Please, come in. My name is Aegirine." He unlocks and opens the shop door.

They enter the shop and are struck by the absolute beauty of the thousands of crystals on display. Many pulsating with an internal light, others refracting the sun in an array of rainbows upon the walls.

Aegirine removes his coat and hat. He hangs them on a three-post coat rack by the entry. A thing of beauty carved from a wood swimming with obsidian black and snow white grain. Its three upright arms are covered with patterns created from the most amazing tiny green crystals. Crystals that, had any of them been paying attention, are the same as crystals in the pendants they wear.

"What can I do for you today?" he says, knowing something amazing is happening before his eyes. "I couldn't help but notice the unique specimen you're wearing in such a delightful way my dear. Are you interested in selling?"

PhD can sense he's avoiding showing any sign that he recognized the crystal. "No, not selling. Or, for that matter, buying. We came here because a wise old woman on Mucus Prime told us the crystal is special in some way. She felt that you may be able to help us unravel that mystery."

His voice drops to a conspiratorial tone and he looks out the shop windows as if verifying they're alone.

"I see. And who's this woman you speak of? Hey! You two. Quit getting fingerprints on my crystals!"

The Guys both jerk their hands back and put them in their pockets. Attention now focused on the conversation.

"Her name is Vapo Rubia. The queen, or whatever she's called, on Mucus Prime," Guy says.

"What an enchanting woman she is." the old man smiles for the first time. "And I understand why she'd send you here. I assume she told you of the legend?

"Yes," they all reply.

"She's clearly the babe," pointing at PhD, "and I'm pretty sure you two are the bozos."

"Hey, I'm not sure we like that!" comes the Guys' simultaneous rebuke.

"Don't take the wording of ancient legends so personally. I'm sure you're capable young men."

He continues, "I can't believe I'm seeing this. In twenty stanyears since I bought this shop, I've traveling the galaxy buying and selling crystals. Never encountering anyone who'd seen one. I'd begun to disbelieve the legend of the Trident Crystals. To my knowledge, this is the first time anyone has seen one in over a thousand stanyears. The time must be near."

PhD's look turns to amazed concern. "So you do know something about them? And what time must be near?"

"Everything I know about them I learned from the old woman from whom I bought this shop. She was ancient by any definition but with a beauty that still shone through. No one seems to know how old, and she'd never say. But the shop has been here longer than anyone can remember.

"I spent my professional career in geology and geophysics. I'd come here on a regular basis to see what new and amazing crystals she had discovered. One day she asked me if I'd be interested in buying the shop. She said her final years had arrived and she wanted it to go to someone who would carry on the tradition. I couldn't resist. I bought it as you see it today. She took nothing but a few keepsake crystals and her crossword awards.

"She spent a year handing over the business. Teaching me how to trade for crystals, identify the real versus fake and how to care for them. Many an evening, she'd sit in that overstuffed chair behind the counter working crossword puzzles. She'd tell me the most amazing stories and her favorites were the ones concerning the Trident Crystals. She'd often muse that 'the crystals are part of the essence of the universe.' She described them in detail but she always denied ever seeing one.

"The legend she told me, over and over, is very old and has been translated from languages no longer in use. The gist of it is that the crystals will be used to protect the balance in the galaxy.

"A time was foretold when the galaxy would be subjugated by beings of pure evil seeking nothing less than complete order. Governments would become efficient and lives would become organized to the point of pain. The evil ones would travel the galaxy imposing this order and ruthlessly usurping control of all the planets they encountered. Making exorbitant fees along the way.

"The legends speak of three such crystals as yours. Handed down for stanmillennia by their protectors to be kept safe. Only to be brought together at the time of extreme danger to the galaxy. Together they're powerful beyond imagination. Though exactly what that power does, or is, seems lost to ancient history. Somehow the three crystals are brought together on a staff or pillar of some kind. Hence the name 'Trident Crystals' and the 'three on a tree' part of legend's little riddle.

"The legends say that the crystals can be given, but never taken. I'm sure you noticed my aborted reach to touch yours? They have the ability to protect themselves and whomever they're entrusted to. Somehow they know things that can't easily be explained by the rational mind.

"Do you, by any miraculous chance, know where the other two crystals might be?"

Before the Guys can say anything stupid, she replies, "No, this is the only one we know of. We were hoping you might know where the other two are." She gives the Guys a conspiratorial glance and they just nod agreement.

Aegirine continues, looking more nervous than before, "I'm going to take a risk. There is something more I know, though it won't be enough by itself.

"The crystals are the key element in some galaxy changing event. The legends say that when all three crystals are together the time is near.

"There is a secret order in the galaxy. They're referred to as the OoD, which stands for the Order of Disorder. They're wise and powerful beyond comprehension. They use their abilities to nudge the galaxy to remain in its proper randomized imbalance."

Guy, who's gone back to enjoying the crystals, joins in, "Great! Now we're getting somewhere. How do we contact this OoD you speak of?"

"That's the hard part. You don't contact them, they contact you. From what I understand, they have some mystic ability to sense where they need to be at any one moment in space and time. The stories say that they possess knowledge of Hyperspace Flies hidden from everyone else. Like backdoors to the entire galaxy only they can use."

Guy is miffed. "So, what? We're supposed to just wander the galaxy and hope they'll decide to pop in for a chat?"

Yes... wander the galaxy...

Guy is barely paying attention because he's so fascinated by the crystals. He hears the disembodied voice. He looks around. PhD is talking to Guy. Aegirine is paying attention to them. There's no one else around. He puts his ear next to several crystals and squints.

Aegirine chastises him, "Hey, no ear prints either!"

Guy pulls his head back and pretends he's involved in the conversation.

PhD tries to calm Guy, "I'm sure that's not how

things will work out. They're righteous protectors with mystical powers. Don't you agree Aegirine?"

"Actually, that's about the only advice I can give. I've only been in contact with them once. It was over fifteen stanyears back. And yes, they just popped up at the right moment. Their ship is the size of a planet and beautiful beyond compare. Such technological advancement as you can only imagine, and then some.

"They saved me from some serious nastiness with pirates as I was leaving a planet I'd been trading for crystals on. They appeared on my ship as if by magic and told me 'Your time is not over.' after they saved my life.

"They disappeared in bands of glowing light as magically as they appeared. Leaving their shoes behind. I never did figure out the significance of giving me their shoes."

He concludes, "I'm afraid that's all the help I can offer. Say, what was that commotion as I was coming out of the shop and ran into you?"

Guy explains, "Oh, that. Just a couple of Helrisien thugs trying to jump us. Probably going to rob us."

The old man's face goes ashen. "Helrisien thugs? The Helrisiens don't rob people for fun. Well, I guess they do. But they were after something and my bet is it was her crystal. If they know of it, you're in grave danger. You must leave Angstuvia immediately!"

With that, Aegirine gives them a gentle shove toward the door. Hanging the 'CLOSED' sign in the window as they go.

After they're gone, he plops into the overstuffed chair behind the counter looking exhausted and frightened. *The time is near.* Keeps running through his mind as he stares at the cases full of crystals.

As they step back out into the street, Guy touches his neck, "FORMU L8? Are you there?"

"Yes, Guy."

PhD looks surprised. "Hey, I didn't know you Guys have subcutaneous comports?"

The other Guy replies, "Oh, yeah. We don't use them much. We don't need them to communicate with each other."

As she's about to ask what he meant by that, Guy continues, "OK. We're in a tight spot here. We have new info on the crystals but we were also attacked by a couple of Helrisien thugs on the way."

"Oh my. That isn't good. There's a Helrisien light attack vessel that arrived not long after you left and settled in right next to the *Thrill*."

"Great! NOT! All we need now is a Pan-Man-Poo destroyer to make this a perfect day!"

"Wellll… that's the other bit of news. Just moments before the Helrisiens arrived a Pan-Man-Poo destroyer settled in on the other side of the *Thrill*."

"FILJAB! OK, here's what I want you to do. We're going to need a scoop-and-run maneuver.

"After you blast out of there, you'll have a short time when they can't see the *Thrill*. Reconfigure her to look like a garbage scow. We're heading to the hypertube station at 6608099th Street East. Can you pull up those coordinates?"

"Yes, Guy, I have them. Fascinating, the street number is a strobogrammatic prime."

"Whatever. There's a large park outside the station. We'll make our way there and wait out of site. You'll have stanseconds to land, take us on and then boost the *Thrill* for the Fly. Got it?"

"No worries Guy, not like we haven't done this before. Though, I still wonder why you refer to the *Thrill* as a female."

The trio takes off at double-time to make their way back to the park to wait for the *Thrill of Agony*.

PhD asks, "So you don't need comports to communicate with each other?"

Guy is so focused on the escape plan that Guy takes over and answers, "It's a long story. But the short version is that Guy and I are able to communicate telepathically. A bit tricky though. I have to forget something and then Guy remembers it. Took a long time to get it working in our favor. Oh, and it doesn't work over galactic scale distances. We have to be in the same star system."

"Fascinating. You two never cease to amaze me."

She smiles and thinks, *This is the adventure of a lifetime. And the Guys are a hot mess of quirks and backstories. Bonus!*

They jog up to the edge of the park. In the distance they hear the scream of the *Thrill of Agony* approaching at an illegal speed.

"Going to get a grak speeding ticket for this one!" Guy laughs.

Just as the *Thrill of Agony* hits the ground in the park, two more Helrisien thugs come out of the hypertube station. They whip out their blasters and start shooting at our heroes as they run across the park to the ship. A blast from the *Thrill of Agony* vaporizes them both.

"Nice shooting EVAC!" PhD yells.

They pile into the *Thrill of Agony*. As one Guy hits 'CLOSE FILJABING FAST' on the hatch control pad, the other shouts, "Get us the phall out of here EVAC!"

They blast out of the park leaving the trees and playground a total disaster.

Now back on the bridge, and panting like tired dogs, the group struggles against the acceleration to climb into their control couches and prepare for combat. PhD has a panicked look as she pulls the weapons controls close and tries to remember how everything works.

EVAC U8 has more good news. "Guys! We have both a Helrisien and a Consultant ship hot on our tail. They're coming at us on angular vectors that appear to have them pinching us off before we get to the Fly.

"No indication they're working together. If anything, it looks more like they're racing to beat one another."

"PhD! Activate main weapons batteries. Guy! Give me full shields aft and all the power the *Thrill* can muster."

Just as Guy is going through the Fly configuration, a blast from the Consultant ship hits them and rocks the *Thrill of Agony*.

"GRAK! Poo destroyers have the frigidest weapons! Sure glad the lovely PhD came up with those shield improvements."

"Oh, it was nothing, really." PhD is humble to a fault.

"Hey you two, focus, that's US they're shooting at!" The other Guy isn't happy.

Luck is with them once again. The captains of the two ships have been so intent on catching the *Thrill of Agony* that they've missed the fact that, at their speed and trajectory, a collision of immense proportion is unavoidable.

Just as they collide, the Helrisien ship gets in one

last shot on the *Thrill of Agony*. Things are popping, smoking and generally not happy in the navigation systems.

PhD watches the collision from her command couch on the main holoskin screen. "WOW! That's going to hurt!"

The two ships hit with a crushing sound, no one heard. They're trajectory and velocity such that they're welded together into a fantastic mangle of Nouveau-Techno-Artos. Their momentum sending them hurtling toward a nearby moon.

– 2^3 –

We've lost navigation and Fly control!" comes EVAC U8's status scream.

With a heart wrenching tone of fear, he continues, "Guys, we're still vectoring toward the Fly and it's opening. This could be a frightening and deadly plot contrivance."

"Here, here, now. A computer is no place for emotions. Pull yourself together and get us detailed status. Deploy MaintMechs." Guy seems touched by EVAC U8's concern.

The Guys and PhD pour over the holoskin displays of damage reports and enjoy a warm cup of Saglath Tea.

EVAC U8 interrupts with an update, "Two MaintMechs have gone critical trying to make the repairs.

"The only chance we have of repairing the Fly guidance systems before it's too late is to inject a tense edge-of-your-seat plot contrivance. Something that drags on in overly dramatic slow motion until it ultimately fails spectacularly.

"One of you is going to have to go EVA to work on an active plasma bypass. You'll have to go without a lifeline. Not because we don't have one, because all this silliness builds such wonderful suspense. You don't have a one in one septillion chance, so the odds could be worse.

"Oh, did I mention you have five stanminutes, fourteen point seven stanseconds to perform your little space ballet?" he concludes.

"Hey Guy let me do it! I haven't saved your life for... Well, let me anyway, okay?" Guy glances between Guy and PhD, his eyes pleading with Guy.

"Look. In case you didn't hear SALIV-8, this isn't a zero-G tennis match. This is an intense and possibly deadly plot contrivance. This calls for a real hero type, someone with plasmic surgery experience, someone who knows how to milk a scene to get the reader's heart rate up, someone like... well... aaaaa..."

He sets his jaw, looks around the bridge, looks around the bridge again, looks under the control console, looks between the lines, and gives up.

"I suppose, under the circumstances, I should set my jaw and tackle this head on!" comes Guy's command pronouncement.

He then turns on his heels and marches straight into one of the two hatches to starboard. After a few stanseconds, he steps out of the sanicube, looks over his shoulder with disgust, and steps up to the hatch marked in bright red letters 'Air Lock'.

The hatch slowly, painfully slowly, seals him from the rest of the crew, and possibly life itself. Through the viewport you can see Guy's face set with determination.

He presses some pads on his sash and configures his Dial-Your-Style to become an EVA suit. He hits the 'Open Slowly for Dramatic Affect' button on the outer hatch pad. The outside hatch slides open at an even more painfully slow pace.

PhD watches Guy through the airlock window. She's biting her lip with a look of total despair.

Guy yawns, drums his fingers on the console and watches pornie feeds in total boredom until he sees that Guy has finally left the ship. He then monitors Guy's actions from the console.

EVAC U8 updates the crisis, "We're now three stanminutes, thirty-eight point oh five stanseconds from entering the Hyperspace Fly."

PhD steps over and puts her arm around Guy. This has a noticeable effect on him, though he doesn't seem any calmer. They watch the holoskin screens with looks alternating between hope and despair. The screens look back sympathetically.

Guy works his way down the hull, hand over hand, toward the rupture. The Fly has almost reached full dilation. He glances over his shoulder to marvel at the distortion of light in the aura of the Fly and the total lack of visual sensation from the blacker than black central portion.

The distraction causes him to lose his grip. He starts to float away from the ship and toward certain death.

PhD gasps, "Oh shit! We're going to lose him!"

Guy catches himself on a convenient plot contrivance, a plasma cannon turret, and returns to the hull.

Guy just chuckles, "Nope, not this time."

EVAC U8 updates Guy, "Guy, time to jump now two stanminutes four point two stanseconds."

Guy concentrates on his work oblivious to the information. Webs of blue green energy begin to lick at his EVA suit. Sweat is dripping from his helmet.

He thinks, *Wow, this is just like in the Sensies!*

His work begins to take on a slurred appearance as though time and motion are not cooperating.

Every movement in slow motion.

Around the *Thrill of Agony*, crimson and gold energy begins to trail from the shields in translucent globs like air bubbles trailing a deep sea diver.

"T e s t   t h e   b y p a s s   n o w   E V A C U 8." His words creep through the comport as if time is warping.

In an odd sensory distortion, EVAC U8's reply comes streaking at double-speed back through Guy's earpiece, "It's too late Guy. Jump in four stanseconds, hang on!"

Then nothing but loud static from Guy's coms.

◊ ◊

Back at the Pan-Man-Poo headquarters, Supreme Commander Cameron heads upstairs to update The Partner on the crash, and subsequent failure, in the Nervosis system.

As he approaches The Partner's desk, he says, "Sir, I have an update on our efforts to capture the pirate scum who've been plaguing us."

The Partner swivels his chair toward a large holoskin screen. A strategically placed spotlight following his every move.

"Good. Where did you save the Obscure-Your-Point? I'll pull it up."

"Uh, well, sir, I didn't take the time to create one. I assumed you'd want to know right away."

"Didn't take time to create one? What! Is my entire organization falling apart? Next you'll tell me that you didn't capture that scum. The last you updated me our Consultants on the ground had them in sight."

"Yes, sir, that's true. The Helrisiens were on their trail as well. Both teams were engaged, but not communicating with each other. Which appears to be where things went wrong."

"Wrong! As in you really are about to tell me you missed them again?"

"I suppose that's the short version of the story."

"Oh, fine. What's the long version? If I may ask and you're not too busy to answer."

"Uh, no, not too busy at all. Both teams tracked them to an obscure area of Paniclateris. Just as they were about to engage, a garbage scow swooped in and plucked them from our grasp."

"What the hell! Do these pirates have an entire fleet of stolen ships? Their numbers must be much higher than the few we've identified to be able to manage so many ships in so many places."

"Yes, sir, your assessment matches ours. They're better manned and organized than we realized.

"Both of our teams gave chase. The pirates had enough of a head start and made it to the Fly before we could disable and capture their ship."

"So the teams are still chasing them?"

"Well, not exactly. As I mentioned, they weren't communicating with each other. They both were vectoring to head off the pirates before they reached the Fly and ended up crashing into one another. Both ships and crews are a total loss I'm afraid." Cameron is now shrinking before The Partner.

"Probably best for them. If they'd lived, I would have had them executed for such a failure.

"Bottom line, Cameron, is you appear to have control and communications issues with your teams." He gazes out the window. "My, that landscaping does look like it needs washing."

"Sir, I assure you I've put in my best efforts. These pirates are not your run of the mill scum.

They're crafty and well equipped.

"I've placed all of our fleet on high alert. They can't show up anywhere without either a Helrisien or Consultant ship spotting them. I assure you we will find them sir."

"Assuming you know what you're looking for. They seem to be able to find a lot of different ships for their escapades."

"Yes, sir, that's a real challenge. However, there's some good news on that front. Our Consultants who were trailing them on Paniclateris reported that there are actually two of the young male pirates who appear to be twins. The woman in our surveillance vids from the Portfolio disaster has been identified. She's Doctor Prudence Hortense Dincheimer. She works at the same research facility as Doctor Piobar. Her colleagues refer to her as 'PhD'.

"She doesn't appear to be a hostage at this point, though we can't be certain."

"Well at least there's some good news."

"Yes, sir. I've also contacted our network of watchers and informants across the galaxy. If they're seen at any port we'll hear about it. In order to keep this quiet, however, I haven't issued a Galactic Search Warrant. Nothing publicly announced."

"Good. Get our folks on the inside at GooAppSoft to tap into the various social media systems. Perhaps they're communicating that way. Or, at the least, posting selfies and pictures of their meals. Perhaps this PhD is following some Sensie star's feed and we can get her location data. Anything that can give us a hint as to where they might be.

"Be careful though, until we have complete control of the galaxy, such activities would be seen as illegal. The last thing we need, at this critical stage of the plan, is to give governments any reason to look into what we're doing. We've invested heavily in keeping them in the dark. That's how I intend to keep them, until it's too late."

"Yes, sir. We're in full stealth mode on this.

"There's one more bit of good news and I'll let you get back to your busy day."

"Yes," looking at his chrono, "I have a racquetball set in just a few stanminutes. What do you have?"

"The latest status reports on the *Attaché* are in. Outstanding work by our Program Manager, sir. She reports that the ship is ahead of schedule and under budget. We'll begin ship wide systems integration testing today and a shakedown launch is no more than a few standays away. Perhaps sooner. Putting us a full stanmonth ahead of plan."

"Most excellent! Now that's the Pan-Man-Poo way. Tell your Program Manager that, if she hits those milestones, she'll get one percent of the budget variance. Make a show of that for the rank and file as well. I want to have morale high as we head into the victory lap of my grand plan."

"Yes, sir. She'll be excited to hear of your generosity. I'll make sure the word goes out in the rumor channels. Best way to make a show of these things is to have the word spread like a virus. For some reason, the Consultants give it more credibility than a formal announcement."

"Yes. Silly but true. Good thinking. You can live another day. Get me a slide deck on everything we just discussed by end of day. Now, off with you."

Cameron hustles out of The Partner's office. That went so well he is frightened to stay long enough for something bad to happen.

◊ ◊

A deep rumble rolls through the *Thrill of Agony* as though the ship is crying out in pain. The lights blinking on and off a few times. Announcing their arrival in a star system which is unfamiliar to all aboard.

"A check of NavBank data shows no points of reference for a Fly in our current location. The NavBank is saying that we need to upgrade to the Deluxe Edition, currently on sale for half-off," announces EVAC U8.

PhD assesses the situation. "Apparently, those energy globules that were bleeding from the shields during the jump caused a disruption in the normal warping effect of the Fly.

"That, coupled with our uncalculated trajectory through the opening, has landed us in uncharted space."

She sweeps her hand across the holoskin she's been studying.

"I see no indication of a Fly nearby. Including the one we just came through, or should have just come through, because we certainly went into a Fly." She becomes engrossed in working out possible coordinates for their current location.

EVAC U8 is doing the same with such ferocity that he doesn't have time to notice that Guy is banging on the outer air lock hatch, which chose this dramatic moment to malfunction.

"Say, you should check into whatever damage is causing that banging noise Guy?" When PhD speaks Guy listens.

"Banging noise? Hmmm, sounds like it's coming from the starboard side. I wonder what that could be?" asks Guy.

"EVAC, ol' buddy, can you ask Guy to check that on his way in for me?"

"Guy's com link is down."

Just as Guy prepares to react to that bit of bad news, the noise explains itself. The blade of a plasmascimitar slices through the hinges of the outer hatch. Guy pulls the hatch back and struggles into the airlock.

The *Thrill of Agony* sets about healing itself. A few moments later the outer hatch is sealed. The instant the inner hatch opens, Guy steps onto the bridge like a matador entering the ring.

He demands an update, "Ok, what's our status? Can we reach a starport? Is anyone going to answer me?"

Too wired from the intensity of the plot contrivance to realize he's still wearing his EVA suit with failed coms, all that the others hear is, "Okda rstu canerch stport".

Guy's demands fall on deaf ears, regardless. Everyone, including EVAC U8, has their attention locked on the image that's just appeared on the long range scanner.

Guy realizes he still has the suit on, hits the pads on its sash and returns to his piratey activity suit.

"Look! A little thank you might be nice, I did just risk my life in an overly dramatic plot contrivance." Guy sounds more than a little hurt.

EVAC U8, PhD and Guy in chorus bark, "Thank You!"

Guy steps up to the scanner, shoving Guy to one side and away from PhD. The image forming is vague but one aspect is definite, it's huge.

PhD whispers, "The preliminary readout shows a craft with mass no less than that of a small planet.

It wouldn't stand out as a starship at all from this distance were it not in free space and changing course."

The distance between them closes as PhD makes calculations and idle chit chat with EVAC U8. Guy is worried and decides that full shield power would be a nice idea.

Guy is beginning to evaluate evasive alternatives. "Look! That mother is big and I don't intend to be caught with my activity suit down."

"I'll have a tactical scan up in a stansec," PhD again whispers from the pressure of anticipation.

"OK, this is weird. The scan is up and it can't see anything beyond the surface of the ship. There don't appear to be any openings on the hull at all. I'm not an expert on all types of craft possible in the galaxy, but whatever this ship is composed of appears to be impervious to our scanners. That just doesn't make sense." Her voice is soft and entranced.

The top two thirds of the ship is green, a lush dark almost black green that overwhelms their senses as it contrasts to the galactic star field background. The lower third is a brilliant white. A faceted sparkle streaming randomly along the entire hull only intensifies the visual assault.

The leading edge comes to a sharp point and is a vibrant crimson and gold gradient with streaks of gold trailing back toward the top of the ship and fading away.

A planet-size penguin is the nearest approximation of the shape. The hull surface seems to be in constant random motion, which makes Guy try adjusting the holoskin screen, then smacking it (sometimes it helps).

When the entire ship is no longer visible on the screen, Guy orders a lower magnification.

To which EVAC U8 replies, "There are no lower settings."

There is a sigh of amazed despair as each realizes just how large the ship is. In what seems like an eternity, and really is a long time, the ship passes across the screen until the *Thrill of Agony* is close enough that it appears as though it's orbiting the monstrosity.

Everyone moves to the viewports to take in the experience. The outer surface is shimmering and so unbroken it's hypnotizing.

"Guys? Remember back at the crystal shop? Did your crystals get warm while we were there?"

"Yes, as a matter of fact, mine did. Guy?"

"Guess I was too distracted until now to mention it, yes, mine too.

"My crystal got warm just before I encountered you two on the *Portfolio* shuttle."

"Are your crystals getting warm again now?"

"Well I'll be a hasblath, mine is. How about yours Guy?"

"Sure enough."

"We came together, they got warm. We were in the crystal shop, they got warm. Now this. I'm beginning to think the crystals know something about our destiny that we don't."

PhD strokes the crystal dangling between her breasts. Her face showing she's in deep concentration. Both Guys are transfixed by the depth of her, uh, her thinking.

Destiny... ahh... yes... your destiny.

PhD, once again, is looking around in panic. "Did you hear that voice?"

The Guys respond, "Huh?"

Before PhD can press the question, a noise rolls through the *Thrill of Agony* like feedback from a gigantic set of amplifiers.

A twisted and bizarre voice that sounds as if it's coming from everywhere at once, "rRfjjlb jHfue BByksuxb, euSkhdjyc uske. Rfkdl xiEEwiv."

The image on the comport holoskin screen is nothing but a distorted swirl of colors surrounding a grotesque and distorted face of some kind.

Sweat breaking in beads across the Langramat console, EVAC U8 works to translate the message.

PhD stands next to Guy and Guy comes up to stand close to PhD. They all stare at the image in rapt fear.

Had anyone been looking at the moment, they'd have seen amazing similarities between the three. But no one is looking.

The Langramat begins to fizzle and smoke from the effort of trying to decode the language.

Another communication arrives, "OOOPS, our bad. Our comport has been acting up lately. Greetings! We are the Order of Disorder Battle Ark *Eudyptes*. Please prepare for your ship to be brought aboard."

The image on the comport holoskin is striking. An attractive and muscular humanoid officer in a skintight uniform. Behind him they see an enormous and complex bridge with hundreds of equally buff crew members rushing about in what appears to be random and chaotic ways.

Guy exclaims, "WOW! Their bridge is frigid!

PhD chimes in, with a wry grin on her face, "They all look like they spend half the day in the gym. They're way cute. We should say Hi back."

"ESCA L8. Give them the standard *Thrill of Agony* greeting. Then give me full power in the opposite direction. Brought aboard my ass." Guy is frazzled from the events of the day.

EVAC U8 begins sending back a message. Their standard greeting is an infomercial about the advantages of advertising on the *Thrill of Agony's* scrolling sign board. A delay tactic that has worked well in the past.

As the engines roar to life, the power across the entire *Thrill of Agony* blinks out. Yes, power blinks, trust me, watch it closely.

What? You didn't see the old cliffhanger ending coming… really?

— Glossary —

Standard xxx – Abbreviated: stanxxx

Hour, Day, Week, Year, Century, Relative Speed. The various spacefaring beings in most of the galaxy agreed to a *standard* measurement system in order to facilitate commerce.   And prevent late arrival at social events.

These are often contracted in use. So a standard century is a stancentury then, for example; stanyear, standay, stanhour, stanmeter, stankilometer (often contracted to stanklick) and so forth so on etc. etc.

Standardized dates are indicated with SY; for example, the current year is *14342 SY*

Space-Standard – Term used to describe both a state of space and the velocity of objects.

As a state of space, it's what would be considered 'normal' space. Not to be confused with Hyperspace which is space that just can't sit still. Standard non-quantum physics apply and objects behave in Newtonian and Einsteinian manners.

As a velocity, it describes traveling at any speed below the speed of light. Speed zones strictly enforced, violators will be ticketed.

Velocity is often further defined, as necessary, into stanklicks per stanhour.

Slur Wine – A particularly popular and excellent wine. Produced on a dwarf planet agricultural colony near Elttaes.

Named for the effect it has on the drinker's speech.

Sisterhood of Relativity – The powerful convent

where only the most endowed physicists are invited to study. Physics is currently controlled and dominated by incredibly attractive females of their respective species. Which, frankly, a bunch of nerdy men really find quite nice.

Physics, in the modern galaxy, is considered pseudo-philosophy and an art form rather than a pure science.

The Sisterhood enjoys enormous social and political power. With wide reaching influence and near total idolization. For reasons no one can actually explain.

They are NOT to be taken lightly.

Sens-O-Net – The pangalactic entertainment network.

Replaced all other forms of information and entertainment broadcasting with neutrino beam transmission enabled by the Hyperspace Fly. Able to carry immersive 3D sensory gratification to match the programing.

Same stupid commercials.

Sens-O-Drama – A popular form of Sens-O-Net broadcast. Consisting mostly of galactic political programming, crime fiction, incestuous family drama and fake judge reality programming.

Sens-O-Cube – A device which, oddly enough, is not cube shaped. Used to experience complete immersion in whatever Sens-O-Net broadcast you are enjoying.

Use is NOT recommended for news broadcasts.

Sens-O-Cast – Name used for individual programs on the Sens-O-Net. Can be used, in general, for any form of Sens-O product. In casual speech, often shortened to just 'Sensie'.

Also slang for the treatment applied to the broken limbs that are the usual result of emersion in a Sens-O-Cube during a news broadcast.

See Also: Infocastcide

Saglath Tea – A delicious compound of herbs and spices noted for its ability to clear clogged arteries and bring on soothing meditative peace.

Do not combine with Slur Wine.

Quantum Anthropomorphic Computers – Often referred to by the acronym QAC. An incredibly advanced neural networked system of multi-mega-ultra-processor computer systems. Capable of passing the Turing Test to the point of being just as annoying as the average humanoid. Used to control virtually any complex technology in the modern galaxy. Specific models are designed to control starships making bridge crew nearly, but not quite, redundant. Crews are still required due to QAC's refusal to make irrational decisions.

Profits – What you get if you sell a product or service for more than you spent.

See Also: Consultants.

Portfolio – A brief case carried by lawyers, artists and other professionals.

Also, for at least a few stanhours, the new flagship of the Pan-Man-Poo.

Pornies – Really? This has to be explained? Yes, they have found incredibly creative new ways to turn boring reproductive activities into entertainment. Three breasts? That's so last stancentury.

Phase Shifting Diurnal Diamonds – A spectacularly beautiful and valuable type of diamond. Valuable because they're actually rare, unlike most types of diamond. They're mined at secret sites near the galactic core.

They have a microscopic quasar at their center that is activated by daylight. The diurnal effect can be blindingly bright and mesmerizingly beautiful. At night, looks like a hunk of glass.

Popular for both jewelry and solar energy collection systems.

Persuasive Voice Techniques – A mind control technique involving modulation of vocal tones in order to alter the conscious state of the listener. Discovered long long ago by a group of monks who wore hoodies that were WAY too large and played with flashlights a lot.

Now taught in way too expensive seminars and used by way too many people, including those damn marketing firms.

Relevant only to the male of a species. Females are born with the ability and require no training to manipulate others using their voices.

Pan-Man-Poo – See Profits

Nouveau-Techno-Artos – An art form in which the artist employs various destructive forces (fire, nuclear, crushing, etc.) focused upon technological items (ships, buildings, etc.). The resulting mess is a transmogrification of mater that evokes the senses with the subtle play of shadow and light upon 3D piles of... uh... trash.

NO accounting for taste.

Note-It-Note Notes – Note-It-Note notes are the main product of the 3N Corporation. 3N is the fabulously successful descendent of the ancient Earth 3M Corporation. They produce a highly advanced form of note taking sheets in a wide variety of sizes, styles and colors. The sheets use a quantum flux adhesive which allows them to be placed anywhere. Not just on any surface, even in thin air or free space.

Also treated with an antigravity coating allowing them to remain where placed regardless of changes in local gravitational waves.

Holiday shapes collection for over one million holidays now on sale near you.

Nerple Device – A torture device often used by Helrisiens. They're designed to overload a victims pleasure centers until pleasure becomes un-imaginable pain.

No, they're not used by the hermaphroditic pleasure hunters. Currently only legal for torture. They were banned for recreational use by the Sexual Stimulation Convention of 13007 SY.

NavBank – A galactic navigational system with Fly-by-Fly directions, convenient points of interest selection and Hyperspace Fly autodial list features.

NavBank reminds you that, in order to have the best navigation experience, you should update often. Like really often.

Always pilot responsibly; at least one eye open. NavBank is not responsible for... well... anything actually.

NavBank is a wholly owned subsidiary of GooAppSoft.

Mood Elevation Station – Referred to as MES. Gathering places with mood elevators that dispense the mood of your choice using any combination of intravenous, drink, smoke or pill form.

Mood elevators revolutionized intoxication throughout the galaxy.

They have the ability to deliver a neutralizing dose, eliminating a huge number of social issues.

That's right, you can be blind drunk out of your mind and, a few stanseconds later, ready to perform brain surgery.

Brain surgery only recommended for actual brain surgeons.

Mediahype – A small planet in the Test Pattern system. Noted primarily for their talents in teaching voice control techniques, public relations and sales promotion.

Mechs (various) – Indistinguishable androids were outlawed across the galaxy following the Hypocrite Wars.

This left a gaping hole in the domestic services and manufacturing sectors of the economy.

Not-A-Droid Corporation seized the opportunity and developed lines of utilitarian (some would say ugly) androids with processing capability limited to their design function.

Thereby eliminating the risk of an android uprising while simultaneously satisfying the humanoid urge to get someone else to do anything that resembles work.

Their slogan has become a galactic sensation:

Tired of lifting a finger? We have a pedantic bucket of bits for that!

The full catalog is available over the Sens-O-Net at the Not-A-Droid netsite: gsn.notadroid.gorp

Don't forget to Like us on FrontalCortexBook.

Common Models:

ServMech – general service duties including preparing food, wardrobe, childcare.

SpiffyMech – the overall line name for a series of models dedicated to cleaning.

MaintMech – repair and maintenance duties including plumbing, electrical, structural.

LoadMech – cargo handling and moving services.

PleasMech – really? That needs an explanation?

Langramat – A popular commercial intragalactic language translator. Used widely on starships for translating comport communications.

Sadly, accuracy is sketchy unless you have upgraded to the latest version. Available for a discount for a short time only. Hurry and order now.

Due to extreme mumbling, Helrisien real-time translations not fully guaranteed.

Just-A-Touch – A well-known brand of hatchway control pad. Allows a variety of entrances including; confident, determined, angry, just upset, calm and seductive.

Caution: They do NOT react well to panic or greasy fingers.

Instashower – A wonderful invention that uses charged particles to remove all traces of dirt, sweat and other nastiness from ones skin.

Guaranteed, 30 stanseconds or less. Guarantee does not apply to Helrisiens and Farlaph Beasts.

Infocastcide – An unfortunate unintended consequence of the wide availability of Sens-O-Net data.

Beings tired of being have locked themselves in Sens-O-Cubes and overloaded their brains with infotainment broadcasts until brain death occurs. Their brains literally turn to jelly. Political infocasts are the weapon of choice.

Hyperspace Jump – The slang term for the jump like way in which the Hyperspace Fly operates. One travels from star system to star system a bit like jumping over the threshold from one room to another.

Also a really hot new dance craze in the fringe systems. It involves dancing to Stuunk Rock on the opening of a Fly. When a ship uses the Fly, the dancers are transported to the system the ship dialed where they continue dancing. The party then continues around the galaxy.

Dangerous for beings over 500 and should be enjoyed responsibly. Do NOT take the purple microdot!

Hyperspace Fly – An immense and powerful device that actually folds the universe to bring two points together.

Resembles a zipper when opening/closing.

Also an incredibly annoying insect that only seems to exist when you're eating or drinking.

Hyperspace – Real excited n-dimensional space stuff where you sit still and the universe goes past you really really fast. This stuff just can't sit still.

Holoskin – A highly advanced form of visual display system. Provides an actual three dimensional visual image. Objects don't just appear 3D, they physically extend outward in 3D.

Used extensively for vehicle displays and available in a headset version. Often used for viewing pornies.

Holoscroll: A handheld version of a holoskin which can be rolled or folded for ease of transport in one's sash, pocket or portfolio.

HoloRoom – Rooms where reality is artificial. Once activated, everything you imagine starts happening as real reality. As if your dreams become true. Sounded good in the planning meetings, didn't work out so well.

Due to the risks involved, HoloRooms were out-lawed by the Reality Maintenance Conventions of 13356 SY.

They were being abused for sexually explicit and high-risk adventures. Resulting in numerous injuries and deaths.

Addiction became so widespread that Reality Return clinics were created across the galaxy. Steer clear. One reality is more than most humanoids can handle.

HoloBoard – Another type of holographic display system similar to the holoskin displays. This device allows the user to write, draw and create 3D images.

Used extensively for excruciatingly long meetings and for scrawling incoherently on in research labs.

Also available in a HoloTable model.

GooAppSoft – Once Earth discovered the Fly, they immediately discovered the FlyCom capability and the galactic Sens-O-Net. It was only a matter of a few stanyears before Google had established a galactic search empire.

Hard to believe, but one thing the Sundbackians completely missed after all the miraculous work done to build the Hyperspace Fly network was a galactic search engine and mapping system.

Google constructed data center spheres the size of a moon in close proximity to critical Flies across the galaxy. They serve up trillions of search results per stansecond.

Seizing the moment, Google acquired and merged with Apple and Microsoft to create a monolithic technology and galactic cloud computing powerhouse.

Anywhere in the galaxy, if you're looking at something on a holoskin, chances are GooAppSoft is involved. The rest of the story will be history.

FlyCom – A point-to-point communication system using the Hyperspace Fly as the conduit. Allows real-time communication across the Fly-connected galaxy. Additional charges may apply.

EVAC U8 – Existential Valiance Anthropomorphic Computer – Unit 8

The tirelessly perfect thing with flashing lights and lots of buttons that does all the hard stuff for our Guys.

Widely considered the most sentient thing on the *Thrill of Agony*.

Eer Weed – A mildly hallucinogenic herb used widely throughout the known galaxy.

Trafficked by the Guys occasionally to pick up a quick cargo run for fast credits.

Name is derived from the sound one makes when offering an eer weed cigarette to someone else, "eer, wanna hit?"

Discretion Shield – With the complete decimation of personal space in the office environment, privacy disappeared. This led to the development of Discretion Shield generators. When activated, they create a 'bubble' of pale green energy around the immediate area. Once activated, no sound can travel through the shield. Thereby blocking out all the chaos if an open office plan and allowing private conversations.

Productivity increased by several hundred percent and overall morale improved radically. Leading management to even further reduce the space allocated to workers.

Dial-Your-Style

Activity Suits: The latest in personal coverings and popular throughout the known galaxy.

The most expensive versions are capable of transforming into any clothing configuration. Accessories optional.

Virtually indestructible and self-cleaning. The creation of which, unfortunately, caused the near collapse of the personal luggage industry.

Hair: The latest advancement in style. A completely digital hair follicle system is implanted under your skin. Most common area is the scalp but it can be implanted under any area of skin where you would like to control the hair.

Hair is grown longer or shorter, colored and styled in a matter of stanseconds.

Unlike the disruption caused by the activity suits, hair stylists were able to easily transition to work in psychiatry. No negative economic impact resulted.

Crabnorvi – More than one Crabnorvus. Dreaded creature of the planet Crabniphera in the dark regions of the Crab Nebula. Frightening beyond description, so I won't try. Virtually indestructible, travel in packs and constantly hungry.

Known to terrorize Intense Attraction Cruisers. Have a gourmet's fondness for spiced humanoid legs. Avoid at all cost.

Couch – Universally being-adaptable reclining seating location. Come in a variety of styles, the most popular being that of a humanoid hand. Available in a variety of both economy and luxury coverings to compliment any decorating style.

Common Models:

Command – Ships and vehicles of all types have at least one of these. Used to control and manage the overall functions of the vehicle.

Control – Ships and vehicles can have many, or none, of these. Used to control various dedicated functions. Such as scanning control, weapons control, etc.

Leadership – These are just big, expensive, over-stuffed and generally adding no value.

Entertainment – Provide personal entertainment experiences including virtual reality and reality reality. Also available in Adult Entertainment models.

Lounging – Just for kicking back and enjoying life. Beyond cup holders, ash trays and oxygen masks not much else unless customized by the purchaser.

Consultants – See Pan-Man-Poo.

Comport – Shortened form of Communications Portal.

Comports can be audio only or both audio and visual. Can utilize holoskin screens in addition to traditional 2D displays.

Subcutaneous Comports are the latest advancement. The size of a rice grain and implanted near the auditory nerve and the jaw bone. Allows the user to listen to and subvocalize communications without pulling out a ridiculously huge device of any kind.

Also known, in some parts of the galaxy, as a rather tasty wine produced in communes.

Bridge – Where all the lights and switches are usually found. Does not allow one to walk over the ship. Seems an odd choice of terms for something that does not go over anything.

AutoCuisine – The latest advancement in shipboard dining. An amazing variety of food and drink can be synthesized from a small store of generic protein and carbohydrates. All leftovers and scraps are recycled at 99.9% efficiency.

Initially responsible for a huge increase in obesity across the galaxy. Now available with calorie control lockout features. Enjoy responsibly.

To fully enjoy your dining options, please update your system to the latest software. Update now and we'll include beautifully crafted desserts and party cuisine for over one million holidays.

Antimatter – That really angry stuff in the power reactor. Oh, forget it, it doesn't matter anyway.

About the Author

E.T. McAllen is not related to the other "E.T.", though you can't convince his family and friends of that.

He has spent decades with some of the largest companies on Earth creating great works of fiction. He's the award winning author of thousands of project plans, PowerPoint slides, Excel spreadsheets and technical documentation. Many of which are fiction classics.

He is currently occupying the spaces in-between and madly working away on the next book in the series.

Quiet please!

Thank you for enjoying another fine
Solipsismia Books publication.